Selected books by Lesley Choyce

The Book of Michael
The End of the World as We Know It
Big Burn
Wave Warrior
Deconstructing Dylan
Sudden Impact
Thunderbowl
Smoke and Mirrors
Refuge Cove
Roid Rage

Living Outside the Lines

A novel by Lesley Choyce

Red Deer PRESS

Published in the United States in 2010

5 4 3 2 1

Published by
Red Deer Press
A Fitzhenry & Whiteside Company
www.reddeerpress.com

Credits
Edited by Peter Carver
Interview by Peter Carver
Cover design by Jacquie Morris and Delta Embree, Liverpool, Nova Scotia
Cover image courtesy of iStock and Dreamstime
Text design by Tanya Montini
Printed and bound in Canada for Red Deer Press

Acknowledgments
Financial support provided by the Canada Council, and the Government of
Canada through the Book Publishing Industry Development Program (BPIDP).

Canada Council   Conseil des Arts
for the Arts   du Canada

Library and Archives Canada Cataloguing in Publication
Choyce, Lesley, 1951-
Living outside the lines / Lesley Choyce.
ISBN 978-0-88995-435-9
I. Title.
PS8555.H668L59 2009   jC813'.54   C2009-903057-8

United States Cataloging-in-Publication Data
Choyce, Lesley.
Living outside the lines / Lesley Choyce.
[256] p. :   cm.
Summary: Sixteen-year-old Nigel has written a class assignment about a world
where teenager's become the leaders of society. Unexpectedly, Nigel's story is
published, and he quickly becomes a celebrity.
ISBN: 978-0-8899-5435-9   (pbk.)
1. Writers—Teenage – Juvenile literature. 2. Science Fiction – Juvenile literature.
3. Time travel – Juvenile fiction. I. Title.
[Fic] dc22   PZ7.C569 2009

Living Outside the Lines

I'd like to thank Peter Carver, trusted editor,
and Red Deer Press for their faith in me as a writer.

To Julia Swan, good friend and colleague,
for her patience and loyalty.

Living Outside the Lines

A novel by Lesley Choyce

Chapter One

"I'm hoping that, one day, one of you will write a novel that will change the world," Mr. Clayton said. He was introducing himself on the first day of the new creative writing class at Northside Regional High. "I'm hoping that this class sets in motion a series of events that results in ... um ..." He looked up at the ceiling, as if he was waiting for a message from above to give him the right words to finish the sentence. He seemed to find it in the upper right-hand corner of the room near the heating vent. "... I am hoping this book, this creation by one of you, is so powerful, inventive, enthralling, and revolutionary that readers take the message to heart and do something to make this a better world to live in."

Norman Wade snickered but tried to hide his amusement. Dale and Steffler just looked bored. I myself wasn't sure if Clayton was joking around or if he really meant it. He had a rep for being a bit loony—a poet with one small book of poetry under his belt. If he was any good as a writer, they said, what the hell was he doing teaching high school? I myself hoped he *was* crazy and I hoped that he meant what he was saying, because I was that student who wanted to write a book that would change the world. Yeah. I was one of those.

I kept this mostly to myself. In fact, I kept most everything that I thought deeply about to myself. Every time a girl would get interested in me, though, I would open up. I'd say what I was thinking. I'd tell her that if we wanted to, we could eliminate poverty, starvation, most illness, and war. We could do this tomorrow if we wanted to. We just didn't have the collective will to do it. We didn't even have the individual will.

I'd say this and then she'd look at me. No. She'd look *through* me. And that would pretty much be the end of that. The funny thing is I couldn't stop myself from repeating that mantra—in one form or another—no matter how hard I tried. Now, I'm not saying it was just the ladies that were turned off by my high-minded notions. It was pretty well everyone. And this goes way back.

So, long ago, I had decided that I would attempt to live outside the lines. I would forge my own path, come hell or high water. The rules were made for everyone else, not me. Not that I wanted to be a criminal. I just wanted to run my own show. I believed in me and I believed that I could do something big. Something worthwhile.

I loved books and I loved to write. I had already written four incomplete novels. Each was 176 pages in typed manuscript form. That's where I always gave up. Page 176. It was scary. But I think now it was all meant to be practice. I was just waiting for the right story to come along. And, of course, the right girl.

Sad to admit, I was a hopeless romantic. I needed love and I needed to be loved. And even that craving could not stop me from saying the wrong things at the wrong time. There was this one time I was making out with Glennie Doyle—I mean, we were really going at it in her parents' basement rec room. She was hot and what she saw in me I don't know—I expect it was because I seemed so mysterious and unfathomable to most everyone around me. Sometimes, it just made girls curious.

So there we were making out and it was all very passionate, but, for some inconceivable reason, I was thinking about what I'd been reading, about diet and economy and global weather patterns and food supply, and I found myself blurting out loud, "It really all comes down to nutrition."

She stopped smooching dead in her tracks. "What did you say?"

I almost picked up my train of thought and was about to launch into what I had learned about the evolution of diet from an agrarian culture to our meat-eating industrial society. But the look on her face said not to go there. "Sorry," was all I said. But that was not good enough. Needless to say, it was the last time I was invited to her house.

And that's the way it went.

By sixteen, you would think certain life lessons would kick in, certain childhood fantasies diminish. Maybe we all want to save the world up until the time we are twelve, and then we discover how much hard work it would be. We get distracted by garbage culture—TV, video games, and bad pop music. We stop reading great books and look for ways to goof off, have fun, cause trouble.

But I didn't do that. I hunkered down with books of philosophy, Chinese poetry, and novels. Endless novels. Not the trashy stuff you find at the airport but important books. I read the classics. Some I liked, some I didn't. I read a lot of science fiction, too. Same thing was true. Some brilliant stuff. Some toilet tissue.

And then this creative writing class came along. I had to submit a portfolio of creative work. I submitted three times 176 pages of my aborted novels. Five hundred and twenty eight pages did the trick.

Mr. Clayton spoke with a passion I had rarely seen in a teacher. "You are a small select group. This is a first for our school. We must not fail. I believe you will all write something of value. You will put one important word after another in the proper order so that it moves the reader to tears first and then laughter. You will pull up out of your heart the deepest of human emotions and you will place them on the page. And you will make that page sing."

Wow. Eyes wide open. The man was on a roll. I looked around at the other less-than-eager faces, the other "select" students. The elite. I thought about ancient classrooms in the heyday of Greek civilization. I thought of the brilliant young minds at Cambridge and Oxford in the seventeenth and eighteenth centuries. But these students beside me did not look inspired. I was sitting near the windows and I could get a view of most of my classmates. Some were still smirking. (Was it *all* a joke?) Some were yawning and not even trying to hide it—this, on the first day of such an historic class. Yikes!

And then I saw her. Second seat from the back on the far side of the room. Her eyes intent on the instructor. I had never seen her before. She was most *unusual.* That's the first word that comes to mind. She had a quiet beauty—not the showy makeup and dyed hair kind of thing. Not the black clothes and ghoulishly angry kind of cute that was going around again. She was different. I studied her.

You know how when you look at people long enough, they somehow know they are being looked at—even if you are sitting in separate cars at a stop light? They feel the vibe. She felt the vibe. She turned.

She looked straight at me. And she smiled.

At first I felt a little embarrassed, as if I'd been caught at cheating or something. I tried to hold her gaze. She did not look away from me. And then she opened her mouth and said one silent word: *Yes.*

I felt something go through me. I no longer heard Mr. Clayton's voice. I no longer felt alone in the world. I felt a little dizzy as images began to form in my head. They didn't make a whole lot of sense to me then. A clear blue sky and then a dome-shaped white thing. A group of strangely dressed young people in a room somewhere, in the future, perhaps. And adults outside, walking through beautiful gardens, looking as if they didn't have a care in the world.

Was it the pep talk from Mr. Clayton? Was it the look from this new girl that somehow inspired me? It was a rough, vague, but highly visual idea for a novel that was forming. *The novel*. The one I would write for the class. The one I would write for her, whoever she was. The one that would make it way past 176 pages. And if no one else in the entire world read it, she would. I would write it for her.

Still looking at her, I nodded my head in my own silent version of yes.

Chapter Two

When the bell rang, she stayed in her seat until the other students were gone. Mr. Clayton was trying to tidy up the pages of notes that were strewn over his desk, although I hadn't seen him look at them once. He seemed a bit dazed and tired as if he'd just run a long race. I was beginning to understand just how seriously he took this creative writing thing. But I wasn't hanging back to talk to him.

I met her at the door as we were leaving. She looked straight at me. She was unlike anyone I had ever met before. "I'm Michelle," she said. "I'm new here."

I didn't expect her to speak first. "I'm the guy who's going to write the novel that is going to change the world," I said boldly. I meant it as a joke—something related to our first moment of eye contact while Clayton was speaking.

"Not if I write it first," she said. She pronounced her words in an unusual accent that I couldn't place. There was something polished and precise, yet soft in the way she spoke.

"You're a writer? I mean, a *real* writer?"

"I don't know what a *real* writer is by your definition."

"I guess it's someone who really writes—like, on their own, like, all the time, not just for some high school English credits."

"Well, I keep a journal," she said, "and I've always wanted to write a book. But I'm not sure if it would be a novel. I have a feeling you're more serious about that. So when you write your book, this one that will knock us all out, what's the name of the author that will be on the cover?"

"Nigel," I said. "Nigel Lukes." It was midmorning break— an odd little fifteen-minute breather for teachers and students that had come into the daily schedule a year ago. Not time enough for much, but we were allowed to walk outside on the high school campus. "Let me show you something," I said. "Follow me."

She followed me out the side door of the school to the small park-like area that had been created by some former graduates. "Look," I said.

There were seven cherry trees there—though they weren't in bloom yet. After all, it was only January. In spring, the trees exploded with red, white, and pink blossoms. But now the branches were bare and black. No one else was there. The other students had gone out the front door and were probably hanging out at the picnic tables on the concrete near where the buses pulled up. "I helped my father plant these. They're cherry trees."

"They must be beautiful. They make me think of Japan—pictures I've seen from the ... " There was a word she was about to say but she cut herself off. "Something from a book, I mean."

"My grandmother was Japanese. My father was the one who graduated from here years ago. He planted them for her and for us."

"It's incredible, really. It's so—how would you say it?—so *not* high school."

"That's why I brought you."

She shivered; then she looked at the trees more carefully. "Wait a minute. My guess is that these are at least ten years old."

"Older, really. I was only three when my father planted them. I guess I didn't help much."

"But it must be kind of cool. To be here now, not far from graduating, and have these trees."

"Yeah, it is." I studied her face. Her skin was an olive color, her hair raven black. And her eyes—a color I couldn't name. Green and brown and traces of blue, all at once. "Where did you say you were from?"

"Well, I didn't say. But I'm from California. Ever been there?"

"A debate competition once in San Francisco. I remember the bay, the bridge, surfers in the ocean. And I went to the City Lights bookstore in North Beach; only there wasn't a beach in North Beach. You from around San Francisco?"

"No, not really," was all she said. "You were a good debater?"

"Yes. But I hated it. I was fourteen at the time. And I thought I knew everything there was to know about every-thing. I had strong opinions and I could back them up. I could argue anything and win."

She gave me an odd look.

"Anyway, we lost. And that was the end of the debate busi-ness for me. Up until then, I had thought I had wanted to be a politician. I had a lot of political opinions. I guess I still do."

"But you don't want to go into politics anymore?"

"No. Remember, I want to be a writer."

"You're really serious, aren't you?"

"Obsessed is the word that would apply."

"I've never known anyone who was obsessed before." She looked me in the eyes again. There was a softness to her, a generosity. I tried to hold her gaze but found myself turning away. There was something else in her eyes. Some kind of pain, some kind of hurt. Or maybe I was just imagining that. Fictionalizing.

"Ever hear of a writer named Charles Fourier?" she asked out of the blue.

"No. Is he a novelist?"

"No. And he's not alive. Nineteenth century. They called him a utopian socialist."

"Heavy stuff."

"Among other things, he believed that all failures result from failing to give free reign to our passions."

I couldn't quite believe we were having this conversation. I had not come across Fourier but I had read philosophy—even the really tough stuff: Hegel, Kierkegaard, Nietzsche, Spinoza, and Hobbes. But I'd never found anyone who wanted to talk about those writers or ideas. Who was this girl, anyway? "Then I'm a utopian socialist," I said. "Where do I sign up?"

She laughed an odd sort of laugh that was maybe not a laugh at all. Then she said an odder thing that stopped me in my tracks. "What do we do next?"

Suddenly I felt like I was in a play. Like we were acting. Like it was all not real. "What do you mean?"

She saw the puzzled look on my face.

"I mean, are we supposed to go back to class or is this, like, a really cool school and we can just hang out here all day?"

I guess I still looked puzzled.

"It's my first day, remember?"

"Oh," I said. "Sorry." I was truly flustered. "Well, I guess we have to go to our next class. What do you have next?"

"Chemistry. You?"

"Math. C'mon, I'll walk you to your class."

We didn't say anything to each other once we were back in the school and in the midst of noisy students. When we arrived at the chemistry lab, she half turned, looked at me in a warm, sad way, and then just walked into the classroom without saying a word. I didn't see her at all in the hallways for the rest of the day.

As I dropped into my seat in math, I realized the teacher was not there yet. Mrs. Schulman was notorious for arriving up to ten minutes late to class. Many signed up for her class just for that reason. And she never really taught math. She mostly talked *about* math and how important it was and how good she was at it. Her tardiness gave me a couple of minutes to flip open my laptop and do a search for this Fourier writer.

French. 1772–1837. Philosopher. Karl Marx hated him, apparently, but the poets seemed to like him. Passion was his thing. And planets. And stars. He had written: *Groups of stars in the Milky Way represent "ambition" while groups of planets around suns represent love* ... and further along: *The properties of friendship are based on those of the circle, the properties of love are based on those of the ellipse.*

What the hell did that mean?

Mrs. Schulman arrived with her mantra, the mantra of almost every teacher in the school: "Laptops away, cell phones off." Ever since the most recent wave of technology invading the classroom, teachers were becoming more aggressive in their attempts to reassert control of their classes. It was a losing battle. Cell phones still rang and some fidgeted with Blackberries under the desk, and some of the new wireless earpieces were so small and self-contained that it was not uncommon for someone like Kyle Mason to be sitting in math, apparently listening to Schulman's so-called lecture, while actually listening to an old Rush album that he was picking up by way of a satellite connection.

That's the kind of world we were living in. Or at least *they* were living in. Me, in my own way, I was a Luddite. A bookworm of the worst sort. A nerd's nerd.

I kept thinking about Michelle. And the more I thought about her, the more it seemed to me that I must be missing something. Maybe she was putting me on. Maybe she was *that* kind of girl. Been there before. Done that. Paid the full fare and got the hat and T-shirt to prove it.

Or maybe she was the real thing. Every writer, I once read, tries to envision the perfect reader. Someone he is writing directly to. Someone like him, but not like him, someone he is communicating his story to in the most intimate way. If—and it still seemed like a big if—this new girl was really who she seemed to be, then maybe *she* was my perfect audience. Or maybe it was all something conjured up by my restless imagination.

Chapter Three

Austin awoke at sunrise on the day of his fifteenth birthday. He walked out onto the balcony and stared at the sun. The sky was perfectly clear and the light pushed back the night, bringing color into the world again. Everyone agreed that the city was better without streetlights. It was good to adjust to the dark nights and be able to look up at the myriad of stars. Not like in the old days when light pollution made stargazing impossible in a city. More people looked up at the night sky than ever before. Everyone said it made them feel connected to the larger scheme of things. The universe.

Austin didn't know about the universe. He wasn't sure he knew much. Certainly not as much as he needed to get on with the task ahead. The responsibility that lay before him. Despite the encouragement of his own mentors, he didn't know how he would be able to perform the job he was trained for. He didn't know what he had to offer. One part of him felt he was way too young to be able to help anybody with anything. He had barely learned what he needed to know.

For the last year of his life, he had lived alone. He had chosen this, although it had been difficult at times. He had moved out of his home, left his parents to enjoy their retirement, and faced up to all the responsibility of taking care of himself, following the rigorous path of his studies. And he had succeeded on all levels but one. He had the professional side of things down pat.

But he had no one in his life—no one really close. His self-imposed isolation of exile had taken a toll. The toll was loneliness. Not that he was ever far from everyone important—his parents, his friends, his fellow students—but he had set himself apart.

I stopped writing at that last sentence and wondered why I chose to begin my futuristic novel, my novel of ideas, with a character who is lonely. I wasn't writing about me, or at least that's what I thought. I'd done plenty of that, written stories about characters exactly like me. No, Austin was different. Yet I knew he would represent a part of me. That was inevitable.

I probably had created a form of exile for myself by being different, by setting myself apart and not trying to follow any of the social rules of my generation. There was a price to be paid for that. For example, here it was, Friday night. And what was I doing? Home alone, writing. But self-analysis was not the way to go if I was going to write Austin's story.

I got up from my computer and went to the kitchen for a cup of coffee. I'd been drinking coffee since I was twelve— probably not a good thing. But it worked for me. No drugs. No alcohol. No cigarettes. Just caffeine in coffee form. I wouldn't touch those hyped-up "power" drinks with all that other junk in them. Give me good, fresh-ground, fair-trade Guatemala beans and that nice little caffeinated buzz between the ears.

The smell of it brewing in the sacred one-cup machine triggered something in my brain. *Déjà vu,* I suppose; but let's be realistic: I'd made coffee before. I'd played this scene out hundreds of times. Still, it was an odd feeling. Hot cup in hand, I made my way back to my room, sloshing a bit of the coffee on the hallway rug. I noticed it landed exactly on the spot where I had spilled some coffee before. Yesterday? The day before?

Seated before the computer screen, I returned to the future.

Austin thought about the six years ahead. Six years, and it would be over, and then his other life would begin. He'd read enough history to know that it had not always been like this. In fact, the six-year tenure was not universal. Olympia had adopted it a generation ago along with Atlantica, the European Union, and Australia. But not Japan, China, MidAmerica, or even Americanada. The old guard in all those territories fought hard to hold onto the old ways. But they watched how well things had been working here, and sentiment in many of those countries was starting to change.

And, hey, after all, who doesn't want to retire at twenty-one and live the remaining majority of their life in leisure? Austin was having a hard time imagining what he would do once his six-year job was over. If he liked his work, why not continue? Maybe the work would stave off loneliness. But by the time he was twenty-one, surely he wouldn't be lonely anymore.

I sipped some more coffee, realized I was telling too much in my story. I decided to leave Austin hanging there in the future. I needed to spend some more time with him in my subconscious. Despite the coffee, I was tired. Some people can sleep with caffeine in their system. I was one of those people. And I had hit a wall in my story when it had barely started. Time for lights out.

My plan was to hole up in my room for the weekend and write. It was like I was exploding with this idea of the story of the future—this impossible place where everything was run by those fifteen- to twenty-one-year-olds. But each time I sat down to write, it was like I was explaining too much. It wasn't a story. It was an explanation. Show, don't tell, they always say. And I was telling.

My cell phone rang. Who would be calling me Saturday at eight in the morning?

"Hi," I said.

"Nigel, it's Michelle."

"Michelle?"

"You seem surprised."

"I am surprised. Hey."

"Hey."

And then there was silence. I hadn't even given her my phone number. Not that it was secret. It's just that she would have had to ask someone or track it down somehow.

She interpreted my silence. "You think I'm stalking you, right?"

Oops. This one was a mind reader. "Um ... no. I was just surprised."

"What are you doing today?"

I stared at the words on the screen on my laptop. I focused on the blinking cursor and then let out a breath and closed the lid. "Nothing," I said. "What are *you* doing?"

"Asking you if you'd be willing to show me around. I can't stay here at home with my aunt and uncle. They're driving me crazy."

"Let's go downtown. I'll buy you a coffee."

"Great."

"You want me to come get you?" I asked.

"That won't be necessary. I'm not home. I'm out walking. I'm about five minutes from where you live."

I almost asked her how she knew where I lived. But I didn't. "You are stalking me."

"And?"

"And what?"

"And ... do you like it so far?"

I just laughed. "See you in five minutes," I said and closed the phone. So my writer's block would have to wait. My beautiful stalker was on her way.

I sat by the window in the kitchen watching for her. When she appeared, I registered again that she was beautiful ... but in an odd way. I studied her as she approached. The long dark hair, the purposeful way she walked. Like she was on a mission. Okay, so I was a little spooked.

My parents weren't even up yet. I left a note on the table saying I was out. Mr. Responsibility.

"Remember me?" she said when I opened the door.

"How could I forget?"

"Ready?"

"Yup. Let's go."

When we got to the sidewalk, I realized she was leading. There were two ways we could have gone to get downtown. Right or left. I always went left. She seemed to know that.

"Where'd you say you were from?" I asked, already knowing the answer.

"California—northern part. Big trees. Mountains."

"Are all the girls there so forward?"

"You think I'm aggressive?"

"I didn't say that. It's just that you're unusual."

"Does it scare you?"

"A little."

"Sorry. I like you. And I think you like me. I think we shouldn't fool around."

We were stopped at a street corner waiting for a light to change. Some older teenage kids were walking our way, looking burnt out and hung over. They'd probably been up all night partying and were now stumbling home. Michelle glared at them, then at me, and shook her head.

"Wasted," I said, after they were past us.

"Wasted is the precise word." She was thinking of diction-ary "wasted," not the other meaning. Suddenly it occurred to me that this girl was just a bit too serious—about herself, about something.

"You never party?" I asked.

"Not like that."

"Is it like a religious thing or something?" My brain was already groaning. Oh, no, she's like some kind of born-again and I was her project.

"Or something," she said. But she was smiling now. Playing with me. "Got you worried?"

"A little."

"I'm a bit opinionated. Judgmental, I guess you could say."

"And why is that?"

"Life is not to be wasted." Again her words sounded odd, the way she pronounced them. And rather formal.

An awkward silence ensued as we walked on. A couple of buses passed us by and we could have gotten on one and had a quick trip downtown, but it didn't seem like Michelle was interested in that.

"Ever think that school is a waste?" she asked.

"All the time. Most of it is too easy. Not enough of the important stuff going on there. I've got high hopes for Clayton's class, though. What do you think so far?"

"I think it will be interesting. Trying to write a novel. But it's just an intellectual game for me. For you it's the real thing."

"How do you know?"

"I saw it in your face."

"You seem to know a lot about me."

"I know a lot about a lot of things."

"Like what else?" I asked.

"Imaginary places. I've been studying the history of imaginary places. It's a kind of hobby. Weird hobby, huh?"

"Yeah, pretty weird. What kind of places? Like Oz, like the Matrix, like Never-Never Land?"

"Yes. And Pepperland, too."

"From the Beatles? Sgt. Pepper?"

"It's eighteen thousand leagues beneath the sea and the inhabitants all love music."

"But it was a really bad cartoon movie."

She laughed again. And when she laughed, it was like her whole body suddenly relaxed. She looked soft and sexy. She dropped the hard and intellectual part that was still spooking me.

"You need to laugh more often," I said.

"Then it's your job to make me laugh," she said.

"Who is your favorite Beatle?"

"John," she said. "Brilliant but self-destructive. Who's yours?"

"Ringo," I said. "Without him, the Beatles would have been nothing."

She laughed some more.

"Tell me about an imaginary place I've never heard of."

"Frivola," she answered after a pause. "Also known as the Frivolous Island."

"Bullshit."

"Well, it is bullshit." She said the word as if for the first time in her life, like it was totally alien to her. But she was still smiling and that was a good thing. "Gabriel François Coyer, 1750."

"Another Frenchman."

"Another Frenchman, and this one wrote about an imaginary place."

"So, it's really imaginary?"

"Yes. There was a real document about an imaginary place called Frivola. The island was in the Pacific Ocean and people there used agates for coins."

"Nice touch. What else?"

"Nothing there was very serious. Trees bent all the way over in the wind like rubber; horses couldn't hold up riders; fields were plowed by women blowing on small whistles and making furrows, and then men just tossed in seeds. Life was easy ... but alas ..."

"Let me guess. Frivolous."

"Precisely. But look around," she said.

I looked at the cars going by, the billboards, the movie rental store, the McDonald's, and the Dollar Store. "So welcome to Frivola," I said.

"Life is too short to waste it on all this," she said, dead serious now. And I think I would have found this remark annoying if she hadn't done what she did next.

She stopped, and took my head in her hands, and then kissed me hard on the mouth.

Chapter Four

We entered the Wired Monk Café and I ordered a couple of dark roast coffees with beans from Costa Rica. We sat down by the front window and I waited to see what she would do next.

"Nigel, what do you believe in?"

"The short version or the long version?"

"The long version."

I sipped the hot, dark coffee. "I believe that most of us operate at about twenty percent of our abilities. I believe that we could achieve so much more than we do. And I believe in spring. Things getting green again. Life returning. I believe in the power of my imagination."

"Do you believe we are all here for a purpose?"

"No, I don't. Every time I hear someone say that, I think it's a cop-out. I hear it applied to all the terrible things that happen. Kids dying of AIDS in Africa, people starving or dying in unnecessary wars. I think, what kind of crap is that? All this is 'supposed to happen for a purpose'?" Nothing like a good hit of coffee to make me opinionated.

"You're funny when you get animated like that."

"Sorry."

"I know what you're saying. It's just that when it comes to individuals having a purpose, then I think we *are* here for a purpose."

"Why are you here, then? What's your purpose?"

She sipped at her drink and then looked deep into my eyes. "I'm here to be with you," she said. Which floored me.

I took the bait. "Who sent you here? God?" I was still thinking that any minute she was going to come out of the closet as some kind of religious type.

"No. I made the decision myself. I believe in free will, don't you?"

"Sometimes. But I thought you said everything has a purpose, like there's a plan."

"We are the plan."

I was feeling a little dizzy again. I'd been slurping my coffee.

Maybe it was the caffeine buzz. I wanted to lighten things up before I freaked. "Boy, you try to take a girl out for a cup of coffee on a Saturday morning, hoping for a couple of laughs, a little goofing around, and instead you get the meaning-of-life conversation."

"Do you want to go back to Frivola?"

I shook my head. "Just go easy on me, okay? The last girl I dated was into *Star Trek* conventions and old *Buffy the Vampire Slayer* TV shows."

"You don't strike me as the dating type."

"What do you call this?"

"I call this the meaning-of-life conversation."

And it went on like that for almost an hour. Then a scruffy-looking university student came in through the door, asked the guy behind the counter something, and then went around to each table, handing out a small green flyer. All he said to us was, "Hi, my name's Gary. I hope you'll read our pamphlet," and then walked on to the next table.

Michelle and I each got a copy and studied it. *Lower the Voting Age,* it announced. *End Age Discrimination.* The name of the group was given as simply *Youngminds* and they had a Web site. Michelle smiled and shook her head.

"Crazy, huh?"

"No. Not crazy at all," she answered.

And then an odd sort of vertigo hit me again. My novel that I had barely begun was about a future run by teenagers. Clearly, there would have to have been steps along the way. I had never heard of the organization. Probably something local, some poli-sci majors at the university trying out radical ideas on the public. Ideas that would never fly. But it still seemed like an odd coincidence.

Gary had dropped off flyers at every occupied table and then he sat down in the back with someone he must have known. As he spoke, you could tell how animated he was about whatever he was talking about. I'd seen other university students like him before, handing out leaflets about globalization, climate change, animal rights. I understood the passion they felt. But the methods always seemed to be wrong. They had a way of alienating the very people they were trying to persuade.

I studied the flyer again, turned it over in my hands. "Do you think we should be able to vote?" I asked Michelle.

"Yes."

"Oh, sure, you and me. We should. But those kids we passed on the street? And all the rest?"

"That's rather elitist of you."

"I know," I said. "But be realistic."

"Some things would have to change, I guess. I can imagine we'd all need to be better prepared to take on the responsibility."

"Is that what your novel is going to be about?"

"In a way," Michelle said thoughtfully. "I think mine's going to be about the future, too. The not-too-distant future where a lot of things are going wrong."

"Dystopia?"

"Yes. And it's not pretty."

"But it's just a novel, right? A good chance for you to vent?"

"More therapy than art, I admit. You're the writer, though, remember? I just want the high school credit for a bird course."

"Bird course? Funny, you didn't seem like that kind of person."

"There's a lot about me you don't know," she said and gave that same sexy look, like she did on the street. I almost wondered if she was going to kiss me again. But she didn't.

The scruffy pamphleteer had finished his conversation. He stood up and pushed the hair out of his eyes, adjusted his backpack—presumably stuffed with his propaganda. Another soldier for a hopeless cause. We both studied him as he left.

And then a disturbing thing happened.

Just as Gary left the café and was standing in front on the sidewalk, he pulled out a couple of his leaflets and tried giving them to a pair of tough-looking young men walking by. They seemed annoyed and tried to wave him off, but Gary didn't want to back off. Instead, he kept talking. Then both guys tossed the pamphlets on the ground. The smaller one grabbed Gary's arms and held them behind his back. Then the other, bigger guy started to punch hard into Gary's stomach and in the face. He hit him viciously four times, then kicked him once in the groin, grabbed the pack, and threw it into the street. Then the two thugs looked around to see if anyone had seen them.

I looked straight at them and they looked back at me. Then they ran. Everyone in the café had noticed. The guy behind the counter had stopped pouring coffee and called 911. A couple of well-dressed adults ran outside to help the young man. I stood up to go out as well. But Michelle grabbed my arm and held on very tightly. "You don't want to get involved," she said. "Not now. Trust me on this." There was the sound of authority in her voice.

She was back to dead serious. I was surprised and a little shocked. There really was a lot about Michelle I didn't understand. I felt like I was copping out, but I sat back down and watched as people tried to comfort Gary as they waited for an ambulance. There was blood coming from his mouth and he appeared to be unconscious.

Chapter Five

All my life, it seems, I'd been wanting to fight restrictions. I questioned almost everything. It drove my parents nuts. I was terrible at following rules.

"You had to burn your hand on the burner of the kitchen stove three times before you stopped doing it," my mom once said. "If I told you not to do a thing, you would do it." My mother was a teacher at an elementary school. She understood kids but I'm not sure she ever understood me. It wasn't until I was thirteen and she sent me to the doctor that she and my dad discovered that I was not exactly normal.

I had always known I was different. I didn't exactly feel

like doing what other kids did. I didn't understand why we were being taught things in school that were so obvious. I expected I was smart. I knew it, really. But there was more to it.

There was this funny little scene, after the tests, when Dr. Rickard sat down with my parents and me. "I've run the tests," he began, "and from what I've been able to conclude, Nigel has a very high IQ, but nothing extraordinary. But his pattern of thought is different from most of us."

My mother looked puzzled but my dad looked frightened. "I don't understand," he said.

"Just relax," Dr. Rickard said. "I've checked a number of possibilities. There's no single label for his condition."

I remember the word "condition" sticking with me. So I had a *condition*. That was what made me different.

"At first," Rickard continued, "I actually thought it might be a mild case of autism. He does have one or two characteristics of that. But instead of it working against him, it seems to work in his favor. You may even have a child prodigy on your hands." This about the boy who had to burn his hand three times to learn a simple, basic lesson.

"I don't know if I want him to be a prodigy," my father said. My father was the king of normal. His favourite saying, when he was exasperated, was, "Why can't we just be a normal family?"

I knew what the word "prodigy" meant but I also knew that the doctor was somehow wrong. I had no great single skill and I could not stay focused long enough on one thing to be truly great at anything.

"I also detected something like ADHD," the doctor said, "but that seems to work for him as well. There were a couple of other labels I tried to make stick but nothing quite did. In the end, it pretty much comes down to this: he thinks differently from the rest of us."

My father looked stunned. It was like a pronouncement that his son was defective. But my mom didn't see it that way. "I could have told you that at the beginning," she said and then paused. "Actually, I think I did tell you that at the beginning."

The doctor only shrugged. "Then we all could have saved a lot of time and money." But he was smiling.

My father continued to look at me, still concerned. He wasn't quite sure what he was hearing and neither was I. Turning back to Dr. Rickard, he asked, "But what should we be doing for him? What should we do differently?"

"Nothing," Doc said, throwing his hands in the air. "Nothing at all. Nigel needs challenges. That's what he needs. But my guess is he will find them himself. He will probably never be satisfied with the way he sees other people doing things and he will want to come up with alternatives. My guess is he will want to make things better. He will try to change things. And he'll run into more than his fair share of walls." He paused and then added, "Like many of us."

My mom had a funny look in her eye just then and said the strangest thing. "The coloring books," she said. "Nigel, do you remember me sitting you down with crayons and coloring books and how frustrating that was for me?"

"I never understood why," I said.

"Because you would never choose an appropriate color. And because you would never stay inside the lines."

"I guess I never saw the point," I said. "I like the outside spaces more than the inside ones."

The doctor laughed but my dad still seemed bewildered, not sure whether his son was going to grow up to be an ax murderer or something worse.

We left Rickard's office and went out to dinner to "celebrate," as my mom said.

"What are we celebrating for?" I asked.

"The fact you are unique, Nigel," she said. "One in a million."

"More like one in fifty million," I said, "if I understand what the doctor said." And then I added, "And that's a good thing, right?" because I suddenly had a feeling of vulnerability. I was thinking life would be a whole lot easier if I was like everyone else.

My mom nodded. "Yep. It's a damn good thing."

My father chimed in, "Hey, maybe you'll grow up and invent something that will make you rich." But I think he was missing the point.

Later, I did my own research into my "condition" and concluded that Rickard was mostly right. There were some of us out there who just had slightly modified brainwave patterns and somewhat different logic. We were always drawing our own conclusions, never satisfied to accept the standard line on just about anything. But, like someone with a true learning disability, many of us learned to adapt.

Let me give you an example. I'd always been creative and I liked to write but hardly ever finished a story. I was never satisfied with my endings. So my stories wandered off into the woods and got lost. They did not end. But finally, in the seventh grade, I had a teacher who asked us to write a story for class. I wrote what I thought was a really good one. I even forced myself to give it an ending. It was about a boy born with empathic abilities who actually experienced what other people around him felt, but had learned to mask his feelings in order to stay sane. In the end, he learned to gain full control of his empathic abilities and eventually use them to help people.

Mrs. Hill handed me back my story a week later and it

had a big F on the top with a note saying, "Please see me after class."

I'd never had an F before. Especially not in English.

"Nigel," she said, "you obviously did not write this story. You *could not* have written this story. You copied it from somewhere. And that's called plagiarism."

"No, I wrote this story. This is my story," I insisted.

She looked at me. She knew I had a history of being rude and stubborn with other teachers, and all the teachers knew about my propensity for breaking rules.

"Then the F stands," she said. "I don't believe you wrote this story."

The story was that good.

A letter went home to my parents. My parents both read the story. My father said he didn't get it but he liked it. He liked it a lot.

"Where did this come from?" my mom asked.

"It came from out of my head," I said. "I was trying to imagine what it would be like to feel other people's emotions— how hard it would be on someone if they were like that."

"Then we should take this to the principal," my mom said.

My father shrugged. "What do you think we should .do, Nigel?"

I thought about it for a minute. I saw the path this would

take. Saw the complications. Realized that, either way, I'd lose. If the school didn't believe in the end that I wrote the story, I'd be considered a real troublemaker and an asshole as well. If I proved I did write the story, and I could do this for sure—sit me in a room with some paper and a pen—well then, Mrs. Hill would hate me for proving her wrong. And, aside from this incident, I thought she was an okay teacher. So I had my answer for my father. "Nothing. I think you should do nothing. I'm going to write another story."

Both parents gave me that look they gave me when I did something that was inexplicable to them. It sure as hell wasn't the first time. At moments like that, they did a lot of blinking and staring at me.

So I wrote another story—a very mediocre one—about a boy who wants to be good at baseball more than anything else in the world. I told Mrs. Hill I was "sorry about the misunderstanding." I did not lie and say I had plagiarized. I would not go that far. I received a B for the story and nothing was ever said again about the empath tale, the really good one that did eventually appear in an American science fiction magazine published under a pseudonym. I even received a check for $250, but I couldn't cash it because it was made out to Willis Yelsel, the pseudonym I had used.

Chapter Six

Austin's bout of loneliness shook his own confidence that he was ready to take on the responsibilities he had been trained for. The technical term was "social engineer" but even people in that profession didn't like to use it. It sounded like mind control or something worse. So they called him a troubleshooter. His job was to try to find things that were going wrong and fix them.

But it wasn't machines or technology he had to fix. It was people. And people were complicated.

The world Austin had been born into was an improved world but not a perfect one. He had studied the history of the last hundred years in

---

considerable depth. He knew that it was the adults who had decided to turn over the reins of power of government, business, medicine, education, and everything else to the young. It was a grand and eloquent social experiment. Leisure—true leisure, involving a somewhat carefree, worry-free, and invigorating, even creative existence—was the goal. Early retirement became earlier and earlier.

A few astute thinkers and leaders along the way had taken a cold hard look at how badly "adults" were running the world. A case had been put forward that the best minds with the best abilities were being wasted. Instead of being empowered in their later teenage years, they had been suppressed or, worse yet, turned over to the media to be brainwashed with silly, banal, and sometimes deadly results. Adolescence, it was argued, had been a "modern" invention and, in times past, many young people had worked, wielded authority, and made good use of their high energy, idealism, and intellect. Their time had returned.

Four years of focused training, and now Austin was expected to step forward and get to work. In another six years he would, like his parents, retire and move on to the next phase of his life. Austin didn't know if this was the best of all possible worlds. But it was his world.

During the years of transition, a couple of generations ago, wars raged, involving even the most educated nations on earth.

Traditional societies could not shift quickly enough to move away from the old, harmful ways. Environmental problems like global climate change and wholesale destruction of species were not being solved. Instead, things were getting worse. The rich were getting richer and the poor were getting poorer. North Americans in particular were clinging to some very heavy old baggage. Some were waiting for a new savior in the form of a spiritual leader, while others were certain science and technology would save them. Instead, the solution surfaced slowly in the form of an idea. And it evolved.

The redefinition of political boundaries helped. Rather than fighting, everyone seemed to be satisfied that the old institutions needed radical change. So the Northeast and the Northwest separated and moved on to the newer forms of society. As did most of the European Union. And parts of South America and Asia. The old forms of government and society still remained in the middle of the continent and the south. In England and elsewhere as well. But they, too, were shifting. And it was widely recognized in the UN and on the streets around the world that the leaders who were reshaping the world were in those countries that had "advanced."

So Austin's was a better world.

But not a perfect world.

The prison didn't exactly have the feel of a prison. No bars on windows. No barbed wire fences. Austin had seen the pictures of older prisons in the history books. If you broke the important rules, you were punished. Punishment was intended to rehabilitate, if you could get your head around that logic. Most convicted criminals, however, came out of prison much more dangerous than when they went in. That had all changed now. Coldclear Facility housed men who had committed violent deeds. Atlantica had a tolerant society—how could it not be tolerant?—but it did not tolerate violence.

Jonathan Krieg stood six feet tall with sharp, piercing dark eyes. His clothes were immaculate and his hair was trimmed short. He was forty years old. And he'd long been "successfully retired," as the phrase went. He had killed a man, his friend, Arthur. Krieg used his bare hands and choked the man to death. Both had been working on research for pain control in their youth. They'd been trained in medicine and had been assigned to research new methods of pain reduction for patients suffering from illnesses that could not be cured. Upon vacating their positions, with years of leisure ahead, the "good years" as they were referred to, they got into an argument. Krieg had actually tried to first kill himself with an overdose of his own pain drug, but when Arthur tried to stop him, Krieg lost control and ended up murdering his friend. Murder was extremely rare.

Despite the intensity of the eyes, which bespoke intelligence, not anger, Krieg seemed perfectly normal for someone his age.

"I'm your new troubleshooter," Austin said.

"And I'm the trouble," Krieg answered. "You're the third one, you know."

"I realize that. I doubt I can do much more than the others did."

"Thank you for saying that. Usually you young ones think you can fix anything."

"Your own work was dedicated to helping people."

"Yes. That's what I wanted to do with my life."

"And you were good at it."

"I believed that pain could be alleviated. I understood that some illnesses could not be cured. Science has its limits. I understood that we had not gone as far with pain control as we should have. You can listen to someone say they are in pain but, unless you feel what they are feeling, you just don't know what it's like."

"I take it you had your own share of pain."

"No. Not really. Not then. Now—today—I could tell you a thing or two about pain, but back then, I could only imagine it."

"And you had the compassion to do something to help alleviate pain."

"Yes. It seemed that the currently available methods for pain control all deprived people of what they needed most."

"Which is?"

"Clarity. Awareness. An alert mind. My treatment allowed people to maintain all three."

"I've read about your treatment. It's still in use."

"None of the younger researchers have come up with anything better."

"You've helped hundreds."

"More like thousands."

"You did good work."

"And should have continued."

"You could have stayed on as an advisor."

He laughed. "Advisor. It's not the same. I should have been exempted from retirement and continued."

"Why weren't you?"

"Because some bright know-nothing sixteen-year-old determined it would be better to turn over my research to the next generation."

"And that was—what?—almost twenty years ago."

"And I've wasted those years. I could have done more."
"I'm sorry."

"You didn't ask me the big question, yet."

"You mean, why did you murder your friend? That one?"

"Yeah, that one."

"Well. Why did you?"

"I don't know. I was suicidal at the time. I was depressed. Arthur was trying to do the right thing. I overreacted. I'd never been a violent person. Something just snapped."

"There's talk of releasing you in a couple of months. Your time has been served. There's recognition for the work you did back then."

Krieg shook his head. "Probably not a good idea. What would I do out there with those other light-headed, light-hearted forty-somethings? I'd just be a disturbing reminder that no matter how 'improved' things are, there's still a primitive side to some of us. Maybe all of us."

Chapter Seven

I e-mailed my first three chapters of *Future Prime* to Michelle for her to read. I'd thought long and hard about the title. It wasn't perfect, but "prime" implied "first" and it also implied "maturity," which to me suggested that when civilization "matured," it would turn over the power to the young. The next day in school, Michelle was quick to respond.

"I didn't expect your story to be so serious."

"It isn't, really. I just needed to keep it grounded. It's meant to be a utopian society—or at least a place much better than what we have now. But there will always be some people who won't be able to fit in. Always some who have psychological problems. So I made Austin a troubleshooter."

"A kid of fifteen trying to rehabilitate a murderer?"

"Yeah. He's gonna have to grow up pretty quick. You start your novel?"

"I did. Like I said, it's set in the future, too, but way different from yours. Instead of any revolution in society, we stay on the same old path. Straight and narrow."

"Hmm. Let me guess. Pollution, war, greed, racism, consumerism, and fear-mongering."

"All of the above."

"Sounds depressing."

"It's not really going to be much of a novel. More of a social statement."

"I'd still like to read it." I studied her face now and saw something there that surprised me. She was quite attractive for sure. And smart. But there was a sadness there and something not quite right.

"What?" she asked.

"You feel okay? I sense that you're troubled by something."

"I just didn't sleep very well. I kept thinking about that guy who got beat up the other day."

"That stayed with me, too. I've been trying to understand violence all my life. Maybe that's why I've got my character trying to deal with a murderer."

"Have you ever done a violent act?"

I shrugged. "To be honest, no. I've been beat up but it was just kids' stuff. Not like the other day. I've been angry, sure. But I'm a pacifist."

"But everyone, if pushed far enough, could be violent. Look how easy it's been for governments to take non-violent, everyday people and give them license to kill as soldiers. And they do it."

"In my novel, the military has disappeared."

"Wishful thinking. But I think it will happen."

I was suddenly realizing that this was the most non-romantic conversation I'd ever had with a girl. I liked it. Someone I could talk to about big stuff. But it was a little weird, too. I gave Michelle a half-smile to break the spell. "Are you always this serious?"

She threw it back. "Are *you* always this serious?"

"No. I have to stop myself. I force myself to stop being serious sometimes."

"How?"

"Meet me after school?"

"Sure," she said. "But we'll have to drop by my aunt and uncle's house first. That's where I'm staying."

"Can't you just call them?"

"No. I want you to meet them. They're a little strange but

I want them to see you."

"Sure." She turned to go to class, but then I grabbed her wrist ever so gently.

"What?"

"You never explained why you are here."

She gave me a puzzled look. "You mean, why am I here on earth? That would take more than a couple of minutes. We have to get to class."

She was goofing on me. "No," I said. "You never explained why you are here instead of in California."

The bell rang just then. She pulled my hand gently off her wrist. "Sorry. We have to get to class."

I hung back. I felt that weird feeling again. A displacement. I was there but I was not there. Vertigo, Dr. Rickard had called it. "Everyone has a little vertigo once in a while. You feel dizzy and it goes away. You just hope you're not on a ladder at the time."

I was dizzy, yes. Almost as if I was beginning to black out—but it never went that far. For a while, when I was younger and before my parents had finally taken me to the doctor for a full check-up, I had convinced myself that I must have a brain tumor but that no one was telling me.

The tumor was why I acted differently, I figured, and thought differently from others. Somehow it was connected to my intelligence, my imagination. I thought my parents were hiding something from me for my own good. I insisted on having a CAT scan but the doctor said, no way. And my parents said it was too expensive. So I guess I'll never know.

All right, all right, so I was a little neurotic. I let the "vertigo" pass and followed Michelle into class, arriving a minute late to creative writing. I dropped my three chapters off on Mr. Clayton's desk. He didn't say anything as I walked past him. The only seat left was on the opposite side of the room from Michelle, who sat by the wall of books.

"How many of you are writing about a character in your novel who is a lot like you?" Clayton asked the class.

Most everyone raised their hand. I did not—typical for me. I didn't think Austin was like me in any way. I wasn't sure where he came from. Or maybe I was lying to myself. If he came from my imagination, at least one big part of him was me. But I would not raise my hand like the others.

"So your character is like you, but he's probably also a bit different," Clayton continued. "How is he different?"

"His life isn't as boring as mine," Barclay Cousins said.

"My protagonist has more problems than me," Gail Tyler said.

"Yeah, mine's really messed up," Dave Greer noted. "He's so screwed up that I think he's gonna tell a story that is really out there."

"Out there is good?" Clayton asked.

"Oh yeah," Dave responded.

Clayton was trying to use this. "What's the name of your character?"

"Dave," Dave answered. The class laughed.

"Dave, but not me Dave. This is the other Dave."

"The dark, evil Dave?" Gail asked out loud.

"Yeah, sort of," Dave said. "Dave thinks he's possessed by the devil."

The class laughed again and Mr. Clayton frowned. I had a good idea what Dave Greer's novel was going to be like and dreaded the thought that we might have to hear him read his stuff out loud.

"Nigel, your character is not like you?"

"Not exactly. To be honest, I don't have a good grasp on the internal workings of my character, of Austin. He lives in the future—a very different future from the one you might expect. So far, I know that he's lonely but he also feels a strong responsibility." I fumbled for a minute, didn't quite know how to say it. "A responsibility to do the right thing."

Someone behind me yawned. Dave, I think, the dumb and ugly Dave—not to be confused with the devil-possessed Dave—and then he said out loud, "Boring." Clayton shot him his own evil look.

Clayton wanted to see if I could take the heat. "Does your character have any internal contradictions?"

. Internal contradictions. What did that exactly mean? "Well, he should be happy, given the world he lives in, but he isn't. Not quite."

"Hmm. He may need more than that. A good character is one with contradictions. Someone who claims to love all humanity but pushes past someone on the street begging for money. Someone who says he loves the woman he is with and then belittles her when she does something wrong. Somebody once said that there are two kinds of writers: those who give you truths and those who give you themselves. What do you make of that statement?"

"I think they can both be the same," Michelle said.

"I agree," Mr. Clayton added. "How many of you want to use your novel to get at some kind of truth?"

A few people raised hands slowly, cautiously. I didn't want to be called on again so I didn't raise my hand.

"How many of you would like to write a novel so you could make a lot of money?"

Dave's hand shot up. So did Barclay's, as well as a few others in the class.

"I hate to tell you, but it's not the easiest profession to make money in. Most writers make very little."

"Then why do it?" Barclay asked.

"That's what you need to ask yourself. Right now, you are doing it for school, but next year, you'll be out there in the so-called real world, and if you want to feed yourself, then you can write, but you'll also need a day job."

"Is that why you're here, Mr. Clayton?" Gail asked. "Is this your day job?"

He just smiled, looked a little embarrassed, and gave us a writing exercise to do—creating a character profile, a character with an internal contradiction.

I found I couldn't concentrate. I kept sneaking a look over at Michelle, her long hair hanging down over her face as she bent over to write. I felt that tinge of dizziness come back over me. And it occurred to me that this time, it probably was most certainly not a brain tumor. Maybe this was what falling in love was like.

Chapter Eight

Michelle's aunt and uncle were just about the oddest older people I'd ever met. Mary wore a long flowing gown of some sort and Franklin wore a striped flannel shirt and short pants, showing off two thin, pale, and bony legs. They smiled in an odd way. At first I thought they were on drugs.

Mary gave me a big hug and Franklin shook my hand and then held it as he spoke to me. "So you are the one who is going to be the writer?"

"I've got a long way to go. But I'm working on it," I said.

"Ever read the novels of Charles Dickens?" he asked.

"*David Copperfield* and *Great Expectations,*" I answered.

"Now there was a novelist."

"I told them about what you were writing," Michelle said. "They want to know if you are willing to share it with them."

"Sure," I said. "It's on my laptop ..." and I was going to say I would e-mail them a copy, but Aunt Mary did a strange thing. She grabbed my book bag, opened it, and took out my laptop without asking. Then she and Uncle Frank spirited it away into another room. I was flabbergasted.

I looked at Michelle. "What the hell was that about?"

"They're a little nuts, I admit. They take some getting used to. They just really wanted to read your story. I had told them about it."

"But it's not that good yet. I'm not even sure where it's going or what it's really about. Besides, it's my laptop. Half of my life is on there."

"Don't worry about them," Michelle said. "Now we get a little time alone."

She had her arms around me suddenly and some music came on, although I didn't see her turn anything on. "You a good dancer?" she asked.

"No, I'm a terrible dancer," I said, but I wasn't pulling away from her.

"Then I'll lead."

"Okay," I said, as I felt her hands slip around my waist and

I followed by putting my arms around her. The music was slow and sensuous and I forgot all about two strange old people snooping through my laptop files.

Michelle put her head on my shoulder and sighed. "I know you think I'm a little … aggressive. It's just that time … well, we just can't waste the time we have."

I pulled back slightly but kept my arms around her. I looked her in the eye. "Why do you make it sound so sad?"

"I can't say. It's just that things will change. What we have right now is something precious. We can't waste it." There was that serious side again.

I took a deep breath. "I agree. We need to live in the present and live it to the fullest."

"So said all the great philosophers," she whispered in my ear. "But it won't be easy. Things will start moving very quickly. Right now, it's quiet. There's just you and me."

I didn't know what she meant and I was afraid to ask, afraid to break the spell. I held her closer to me, tried to keep my feet shuffling vaguely in synch with the music. I closed my eyes briefly and then opened them and scanned the room. There were no family pictures on the wall. The furniture all looked new. The house had a funny unlived-in quality.

We danced for a while—if you could call that dancing—and even as we sat down on the sofa, I still felt the imprint of her body against mine. The music stopped of its own accord and Frank burst back into the room and tossed my laptop down on the cushion beside me. "You want a beer?" he blurted out to me.

"Uncle Frank," Michelle said, seemingly shocked, but smiling. "You're not supposed to offer beer to someone underage."

"We need to celebrate," he said

"Celebrate what?" I asked.

"Your story. It's going to be great. You haven't fully found your voice but it's getting there. How about that beer?"

"Sure," I said.

Mary came back into the room now and smiled at me, but didn't say a word. She had a kind of serenity about her, in contrast to her husband. She looked directly into my eyes as if she had known me for a long time, which made me a little uncomfortable.

Frank nearly ran to the kitchen, came back, and handed me a can of beer. He was sure worked up about something. When I popped the metal tab, the shaken beer foamed up out of the can and I sucked on it to keep it from slopping over me and the furniture.

"I hope you don't mind," Mary announced matter-of-factly, "but Frank has already posted those first three chapters of your story on his Web site."

"What?" Michelle asked.

Frank threw up his hands. "Sorry. I should have asked but I got carried away."

I felt violated. My personal space invaded. "You had no right to do that," I said indignantly.

Frank seemed surprised at my reaction. He blinked a couple of times and then said with real enthusiasm, "But it was great. I felt I had to share it. You shouldn't keep a story like that to yourself."

"If they like it, you'll have to give them more," Mary added, looking directly into my eyes again.

"Who are *they?*" I asked.

Frank smiled and opened his own beer. "Cheers," he said, holding his can aloft. "*They* are the people who visit my site. Probably just a handful of old geezers like me, looking for new ideas, new talent."

I tried to get over the fact that something really weird had just happened, but as I sipped my beer I thought, what the hell. What did I have to lose?

Michelle was sick for three days, which she said was common for her. She missed a lot of school, saw a lot of doctors, but it was nothing I should worry about, she said. But I did worry. I had fallen in love with the girl. And I was pretty sure it was the real thing.

Her Uncle Frank had forwarded to me e-mails from people who were reading my novel excerpt on his Web site. I checked out the site and it had the most bizarre mishmash of theories and ideas posted. Mostly crackpot stuff—plans for anti-gravity devices, discussions of perpetual energy machines, proposals for communal living, and rants about how to change the world by eating only beans, lentils, and rice.

But whoever they were that visited the site, they liked my story. And they said so. Clearly, I could be a hero to the lunatic fringe and that felt good. I kept writing, and a week later, I posted more of *Future Prime* on Frank's Web site.

Not long after that, I got an e-mail from Gary, the guy we saw get beat up. He had read my writing on the nutso Web site and tracked me down.

"Meet me at the coffee shop, dude. 4:30 Wednesday. We need to talk."

Gary had some bruises on his face. He was sipping a cappuccino when I arrived. I was a little nervous.

"Dude," he said, "thanks for coming."

"Hey. No problem."

He had a lot of nervous energy. The guy seemed totally wired. "I've seen you before, right?"

"I was here the day you got beat up. You gave me a pamphlet."

"Did you read it?"

"Yeah. Something about lowering the voting age."

"Lowering the everything age," he corrected.

"Why? What's the big deal?"

"The big deal is we're wasting ... we're wasting you and people like you."

"I don't feel like I'm missing much. Hey, so I can't vote."

"Like I said, it's not just voting. What else can't you do?"

"Can't drink. But I guess I could if I wanted to. No big one either." I was thinking of the beer Michelle's uncle had given me. It was an odd thing for an adult to do.

Gary's hands were fidgeting in the air in front of him. "You gotta look at the big picture," he said. "The really big picture. It's in the history. Childhood was invented in the 1800s. You want a coffee? What do you drink?"

"Dark roast," I said.

He jumped up from the table and went to the counter. I pondered what the hell he was talking about. I wondered if I should be hanging out with this guy at all.

He returned with my coffee. "How old are *you?*" I blurted out.

"Twenty-one."

"Then what are you worrying about? You're a freaking adult." I guess I was sounding defensive and I didn't exactly know why.

"Nigel, I'm thinking about the future. And the past. Down through the years, rights have systematically been taken away from the young. So-called laws created to protect kids have instead imprisoned them. *Youngminds* is all about setting you free."

Some things were beginning to click. "And that's what you liked about my story?"

"Your story is a bit weird. I didn't get it at first. I mean, why was Austin so lonely? Why was he so uncertain? And why was he working with a murderer in a world that should have been a utopia?"

"I'm not sure I even have answers to that yet. But he's the character who dropped into my head. It's his story and I have to see it through."

"I know why, Nigel. Do you want me to tell you?"

"No," I said, feeling a little spooked and a tad resentful. "It's my story, and how it goes is none of your business."

"Right," he said, backing off.

I sipped my coffee. "Why'd those guys beat the crap out of you?" I asked.

"Oh, right. You were here. Them. I'm not sure I know. All I did was ask them to read the pamphlet."

"You were a little pushy," I added.

"A tad. But I didn't think they'd jump me. Man, that sucked."

"They must have felt threatened."

"Doesn't seem logical, does it? But you're probably right. They resented the fact that I wanted to change something."

"You want twelve-year-olds voting for presidents and prime ministers, right?"

"I didn't exactly say that, but one day, sure. Why not?"

"And in my novel, we're already there. But that's just fiction."

Gary smiled. "Fiction, yeah. But you don't think fiction changes the way people think?"

"So far it's just a fragment of a story. And so what; it's on the Internet. Anybody can post anything on the Net. One day it's a big deal; the next, it's ancient history."

"Right. And that's why I want to help you to get it published."

"As a book?"

"Yes. A book. It's what you want, right?"

"That will never happen," I said. "That's ridiculous."

"How do you know? Why don't you let me help you?"

I still didn't trust this guy. "You may not like where the story goes. Heck, I don't even know where it's going. It may go nowhere."

"Nigel," Gary said, taking a deep breath, "I'm just a link in a chain. You are just another link in a chain. Yet, we're both important. We're part of a process. If history teaches one thing, it's that you never ever know what the result of a single action can be. You might be able to observe the immediate effect but not the ultimate outcome."

I still didn't trust him. A history major at university, for sure. An activist who viewed himself as a radical. And then he said something that really pissed me off.

"Nigel, you have this purpose, man. You have this gift— this writing thing. You need to finish your novel and put it out there. You need to see it through. You have no choice."

It could have been his tone of voice. But it was almost like a threat. No wonder those guys on the street got angry.

"No. I do have a choice. I'm going to pull my chapters off the Internet. I'm going to finish my writing project for school and that will be the end of it. So just back off and leave me alone, okay?"

I got up to go and Gary grabbed my wrist. I looked him straight in the eyes. I was almost ready to slug him myself. And that was not like me at all. He let go. I turned and left, deciding I'd find another coffee shop to hang out at. Right then, I wasn't sure I wanted to finish my novel at all. It was just getting a little too weird.

Chapter Nine

Three months into his work with Jonathan Krieg, Austin felt he was getting nowhere. He was certain he had chosen the wrong profession. He was depressed and recognized the symptoms. An appointment was made with his own troubleshooter—nineteen-year-old Jocelyn Quaid. Jocelyn was professional and confident. Everything that he wasn't.

"You're not alone," she said. "Fifteen is a rough age. Always was, always will be."

"But it's not like what we've been told. I'm not ready for this."

Lesley Choyce |

She smiled. "That's what it feels like now."

"That's what it is now."

"You chose a difficult profession. You could have picked something easier. What you need to do is work through this. The doubt is part of the learning curve."

"Bullshit."

She smiled again. Austin couldn't help noticing that she had a flirtatious look about her.

"I haven't heard that word for a while. Not since yesterday, in fact."

"I can't help Krieg. What is it again I'm supposed to do? Cure him? Make him not hate himself?"

"Yes. And prepare him to return to society."

"Right. It's not like the old days. We let murderers go free now. No more capital punishment. No more life sentences."

"Neither was ever a deterrent for murder. Krieg suffered some kind of breakdown. He was a great humanitarian. If we can help him, then we help all of us."

"But why did they assign someone just out of training. Why me?"

"Because the others had failed. The others had been experienced. All close to retirement. You are an experiment."

"The blind leading the blind."

"Precisely."

"What if I fail?"

"Then we all fail. In fact, no one is all that confident that you will succeed."

"Then it's all a joke."

"No, it's not a joke. It's an attempt to move beyond what we know."

"But look at me. I have no social life. I'm lost and lonely. I can't help anyone. I can't even help me."

"You think you are the first fifteen-year-old to express those feelings?"

I shook my head. "But that doesn't make it any easier."

"Jonathan Krieg is what's left over of the old ways. It's not like we've eradicated human violence. But things are better."

"What if this whole damn social experiment fails?"

"It's not failing. Even the reluctant countries are starting to lean our way."

I studied her. "How many more years do you have?"

"Two," she said. She knew what I meant. "And then I advance."

"You retire?"

"No one really retires. We relinquish our responsibilities. We are always there to counsel the young."

I'd heard that line plenty of times before. "When my parents turned thirty they abandoned me. Like the others. That hurt."

"They didn't really abandon you. You still lived with them. They *allowed you to begin to explore your full potential."*

"Bullshit. Cut the textbook crap."

"There's that word again. But you know what I mean."

"I think I want the retraining. I'd prefer a job where I work with numbers, not people."

"And you think that will make things better for you?"

"I don't know."

"Give it another month. Talk to Krieg about this. He needs to know who you really are and what you feel. After him, there will be others. If you decide to stay with the troubleshooting job."

Austin let Krieg teach him chess and then a Japanese strategy game called Go. He stopped trying to offer him any form of therapy at all. That was his new strategy. He gave up trying to help and decided to be Krieg's friend. It made Austin feel like a charlatan. But it also made him feel better.

"Maybe suffering is the teacher," Jonathan said to him one day. "That's what I had learned from my work in pain control. I never

believed suffering was a noble thing for any of us. But it was a necessary thing. A life without pain is a life without growth."

Austin had been putting himself to sleep at night by reading classic novels. He read All Quiet on the Western Front and was appalled by the horrors of trench warfare in World War I. It was a moving and terrifying account that revealed the true inhumanity of war. Anyone would have thought that this single book alone would have prevented Europeans from ever going to war again. It had been widely read in many languages. But it did not stop Germany from re-arming and forcing Europe into another bloody war.

After that, he read Catch 22 and then The Things They Carried.

But now Austin lived in a world that did not invest its money in arming for war. Diplomacy and goodwill had replaced weapons and soldiers. Some older citizens still thought this naïve, but they were no longer the ones making decisions. In fact, part of the success of the restructuring of the workforce was due to the infusion of young people back into productive jobs rather than training them for war.

A week had gone by since his meeting with Jocelyn. And then a month. Austin had not quit his job. And he had been assigned two more cases of violent offenders. Both had gone from resistant and angry to relaxed and even chatty. But Austin confessed to his boss over and over that he didn't feel like he was doing anything that was in any way professional or based on what he had learned in his training.

He stopped reading war novels and he went out at night to a coffee shop where, one rainy evening, he met a seventeen-year-old teacher named Tamara. Although neither called it dating, they began to meet there on a regular basis and talked about absolutely everything there was to talk about. They were drawn together, they both admitted, out of their mutual loneliness, but Austin soon grew to appreciate her quiet beauty and her understanding of the world and people. And he was beginning to feel a deep longing to be with her more and more, although he could not bring himself to say this out loud. Instead, their conversations were often about their work.

"The big trouble with teaching kids today," she said one day, "is that they have no real concept of the past. Everything changed so quickly. They don't have any idea how life was before the change. They have it easy but it doesn't seem easy to them. We have to teach them on their terms, not ours."

"You make it sound like you remember what it was like before the change."

"I don't really remember. But I'm a history teacher. So I studied it. And remember, the transition took over fifty years."

"Ever look into issues of crime and punishment in the early twenty-first century?" Austin asked.

"Not really," she said.

"It was still very primitive. Between 1977 and 2000 there were 683 executions in the U.S. Lethal injections, electric chairs. It all seems pretty barbaric. Instead, now you have a fifteen-year-old boy trying to help an adult murderer reform. And he's not sure he knows what he's doing."

"I felt that way when I started teaching," Tamara admitted. "And I had some very difficult eleven-year-olds—some with real problems. And they all thought they were smarter than me. That's the tough part about teaching. We think we know what we're doing because we are older—we've been trained. But they know they will be in our shoes in just a few more years. They think they're ready for more responsibility. They don't always like authority."

"Kids never did." Austin had a puzzled look on his face now. "But maybe we're missing something. That's the way it feels to me. Like something has been taken away."

"Like your childhood? Your innocence? Your play time?" She said the last word in a mocking tone.

"Precisely."

"That's what they did."

"Who?"

"The ones who changed things." Tamara was back to being the history teacher now. "It started in the early twenty-first century. When all those murderers were still on death row. Ideas started floating around. There was that second war in Iraq lingering on and it looked like a third one coming up in the Middle East. And Afghanistan was going nowhere. And then the economy started to slide, and all the confusion broke out in China, and the food shortages. Climate change. People started thinking that the decision-making was very bad. Hey, I mean, converting food sources into fuel for cars instead of food for starving people? Come on."

"But it wasn't us who brought about the change. I mean, it wasn't teenagers who totally rebelled and took over."

"No. It wasn't. Once the ball was in motion, it was the older people—not even the ones in their twenties, but the older ones.

Thirty and over. They saw the writing on the wall. Change now or face the consequences."

Austin looked at her and suddenly realized how much wiser she was than him. "So they sacrificed their children?"

"Yes," she said. "They didn't have to make any Biblical kind of offering to God. They decided we were ready. In some ways they were turning things back rather than forward. Like you say, they took away play time. They told us we had to grow up more quickly, that we were capable. They set us up and then gave us the keys to the kingdom."

And then Austin said out loud what he had been feeling ever since he had started working. "But I just don't know if I'm ready for what I'm doing. I don't know if I'm capable of doing my job."

Tamara looked deep in his eyes, then leaned across and kissed him with such tenderness and passion that Austin thought he had died and gone to heaven.

Tamara lived in an apartment that overlooked the sea. Austin visited her on weekends and stayed over whenever she asked. They slept together but didn't have sex. To them this seemed quite normal. On Tamara's eighteenth birthday, Austin bought her an eighteen-speed bicycle. He bought one for himself as well. Now she was eighteen and he was still fifteen. It seemed like a massive age difference but he thought he loved her. Riding their bikes out into the countryside around the city, along the coastal highway, they felt free and young. The first time they made love was in a spruce forest, on a blanket by the edge of the sea. They were lying naked in a pool of sunlight in the forest surrounded by ferns and forest. It was the happiest Austin had felt in his relatively short lifetime.

"What would happen if we just disappeared?" Austin asked Tamara afterwards.

"Nothing. We could go south and live in a place where the adults still run things. We'd have a few good years before we were fully like them."

"Would you do this with me?" Austin wasn't one hundred percent serious.

"I don't know."

"Others have done it."

"Sure. The older ones who don't like turning over the work to the younger ones. Sometimes they're not satisfied, though. Sometimes they come back."

"And sometimes they stay," Austin countered.

"But I don't think I could do it. What would my students think? I'd feel like I was giving up. What would happen if we all gave up?"

"I don't know," Austin said, leaning up on one elbow and looking deep into Tamara's eyes. "It was just a fantasy, I guess."

Chapter Ten

Michelle and I were walking through the park near the harbor. Workmen were chain-sawing some of the trees that had blown over in a big blast of a storm last fall. The forest had been decimated and it would take years to recover.

"I don't understand why your protagonist seems so dissatisfied," Michelle said. "He seems to be fighting something."

"He doesn't understand what he's doing, or the world he lives in."

"Isn't that always the case for people our age?"

"I don't know. Is it?" I asked.

"Knowledge can be defined as the loss of innocence.

Responsibility is the loss of freedom."

"I'm starting to see that. I'm starting to have some serious doubts about this novel. Since your uncle posted those chapters, I've been getting some pretty weird e-mails. And that thing with Gary. It's like I've stumbled into something."

Michelle suddenly looked quite upset. "Nigel, you have to finish it. People need to read it."

"What would be the big deal if I didn't? Flunk the class, maybe. Mr. Clayton would be disappointed. I could take an extra credit next year."

"You've been working on it for over three months. You can't give up."

"Well, my other school work has been sliding. I don't know. And my parents are saying I'm acting weird."

"You said your parents have been saying that since you were little."

"True. But they're right. Maybe I should try to be more normal."

"Normal would be boring. I wouldn't like you if you were normal."

"Really?" I asked, my feelings hurt.

She smiled and ran her fingers through my hair. "Don't worry. You'll never be normal."

"Here," I said. I handed her a memory stick that was hanging from a strap around my neck. It had the recent chapters of *Future Prime.* "There's a girl in it now. Kind of a love interest."

She took the memory stick and looped the strap around her neck, tucked the stick itself down inside her shirt where it hung between her breasts. That gave me a warm feeling inside.

"It's going to be a short novel—fifty thousand words."

"A novella."

"I guess you can say that. I'll finish it before the school year is over. I have to. If I stay there too long, in the story that is, it will drive me nuts. I think it's already driving me nuts. It's way too real. And it's not going in the direction I thought it would go. I thought I was writing a utopian novel. But my main character is questioning the world he lives in."

"Questioning is always a good thing. But you won't give up?" She was holding onto my arm now and I couldn't help but touch the smooth skin of her face. As I looked in her eyes, though, I saw something funny. A shifting of focus. And she suddenly seemed short of breath.

"You all right?"

"I think you just made me feel funny," she said. I should have taken it as a compliment but it worried me.

"You look pale."

"I'm okay," she said and she clenched her hand around the memory stick as if it was a locket I had given her. Something

Lesley Choyce |

romantic. "Can I show my uncle the chapter if I like it?"

I was going to say no. But with her hand to her chest like that and the woozy soft look in her eyes I couldn't resist. "Why not," I said. "Sure. Let the wackos find me. I can handle them."

As I was walking her home, though, she felt disoriented and we sat down on somebody's lawn. She suddenly took a deep breath—and then passed out, slumping forward onto me. I was so scared. All I could do was hold her for a second or two, my mind frozen. I put my ear to her mouth and knew that she was still breathing. And then I noticed the bracelet she was wearing. Some kind of medical alert? I wondered. I looked at it but it had symbols and no words. I pulled out my cell phone and was about to call 911 when she took a quick deep breath and opened her eyes. She was confused.

"You scared me," I said.

She tried to shake it off. "Sorry. I fainted."

"Yeah, you did. What was that?"

"It happens from time to time."

"But you're okay now?"

"Yes."

I held out her wrist. "What is this?"

She quickly covered it with her sleeve. "I'm sorry. I'll explain sometime. Could you just walk me home now?"

"Sure."

They say there are certain points in your life where you take a step and there is no turning back. A point of no return. I think the memory stick was my point of no return. By that evening, crazy Uncle Franklin had posted my chapters. There were a total of seven chapters on the Internet now. I had told myself I wouldn't even go to that site or look at any of the comments posted, but I started to get several dozen Google alert messages and discovered my novel was being copied and posted on sites all over. And then the personal e-mails started again.

I read the first twenty and then I just started deleting them. Dozens of them. At first it was just "fan mail," some of it even from sixteen- and seventeen-year-old girls—at least they claimed to be girls. But then I started hearing from the critics. One guy wrote: *Your story is bullshit, man. You have no idea what you are talking about.* Another one said: *If we let kids run the world, they wouldn't fix it, they'd destroy it.* Something that I was writing was scaring them. I couldn't see why they would care or bother. I didn't answer my critics but I was tempted to answer the fan mail, maybe ask for pictures. But I didn't. I was working on this thing with Michelle. She wasn't like any girl I'd ever met.

If I had fallen in love before, I could have compared what I was feeling now to what I had felt before. But I hadn't fallen in love before. I'd been attracted to girls and girls had been strangely attracted to me. But it was never mutual. We were always out of synch. I liked the girls who thought I was a geek, and the girls I had no interest in were attracted to me. The potential of unknown Internet girls did nothing for me. Michelle seemed to have no interest in anyone other than me as well. I didn't understand that. Other guys would try to get her attention but she seemed to be able to give them a look or say a few words and they were history.

Mr. Clayton's class was going poorly. Despite his best efforts, he was coming to the realization that he had a class of lazy, non-creative students who failed to hand in work on time or put any serious effort into their fiction. Even Michelle seemed pretty matter-of-fact about her own writing. She did the work—writing her own novel about a truly dystopian future where countries engaged in weather wars, old men still ran nations, and old rules still applied. The focus was on an unhappy middle-class family. The narrator was a nerdy twenty-one-year-old university student who was on medication to keep her from depression. She showed it to me and I never said a bad word, but there wasn't much of a story, and her protagonist just seemed plain unhappy and surrounded by other unhappy people who felt the whole messed-up world was beyond repair. Clayton was giving her "B" grades for her work and that was a bit of a gift.

Clayton himself seemed to be sliding into a kind of depression. He had less enthusiasm for anything during class and sometimes resorted to asking us to work on our novel during class. During that time, many of my classmates preferred to pick their respective noses, check their text messages, slip some doctor-prescribed medications into their mouths, gossip to each other in whispers, or simply put heads to desks and fall asleep. Anyone observing this group, once considered, by Clayton, at least, to be the best and brightest, would have undoubtedly come to the conclusion that, if this represented the future, then a dismal future it would be. Probably just like the one described in Michelle's novel.

It was a month before the end of school when Clayton suddenly seemed cheerful and his old self—buoyant, full of nervous energy, broadly smiling. He chortled on with great enthusiasm as he had in the early days of the term about how in fiction, "all things are possible." And his borrowed favorite: "Never let the facts get in the way of the truth." I was disappointed that it was one of those many days when Michelle was out sick.

"Nigel, can I see you after class for a few minutes?"

Clayton said after the ringing of the bell.

I hung back, happy to have a chat with him, and hoping I could miss math altogether. I sat down at a desk in front of Clayton as he smiled some more and made a little tent with his fingers in front of him.

"You look pleased about something," I said.

"I am. Although I may have overstepped my bounds."

"What do you mean?"

He looked a little guilty. "I showed your novel-in-progress to a publisher friend. William Botzweiler at Twin Bridges Press."

I shrugged and threw up my hands. "Hey, it's all over the Internet. Turns out I'd be in deep shit with my fans if I didn't finish it. And if I do finish it, I have creepy enemies who want to break my legs."

"I know. I've been checking a few blogs. It's quite amazing really. The strong opinions."

"I know it's not that great. It's just that I seem to have hit some kind of nerve."

"Yes. You did. That's what Bill said. The editor. He said he wants to read the whole thing. I think he wants to publish it. He may even be willing to give you a contract to finish it. He was pretty excited."

"Publish it?"

"As a book. Twin Bridges is a small press but it's owned

by one of the big international publishers. His specialty is finding a book on a 'hot topic' and fast-tracking it into print. There's a lot of discussion about youth rights, as you know. Pretty heated stuff. Guess he thinks your book would play right into it."

"Wow." My first reaction was that this was too good to be true. But I was thinking about Gary and his campaign. Apparently there were a lot of Garys out there. It was a big issue. "I thought you said something like one in a thousand manuscripts gets published. That it's so competitive."

"It is. You're that one in a thousand." Clayton was beaming.

"But it's not even finished. In fact, I think it might be off the rails."

"It's not off the rails. You have an uncertain and confused protagonist. Better to view things from his point of view than from someone who buys into the utopia thing. But Bill made it clear, he wouldn't market it as science fiction. That's too narrow. And it wouldn't be a young adult novel. He wants it to be what it is: controversial. He said he'd be willing to offer a serious advance."

Suddenly it occurred to me that this was too quick, too good. "Advance means money, right?"

"Advance against royalties. You get some money up front and you make more after a while if the book keeps selling.

You get paid for every book sold."

"I hadn't even been thinking about money."

"It's publishing. It's a business."

"And he thinks the book is that good?"

Clayton was squeezing his hands together. He seemed to be having a hard time holding back his enthusiasm. He cleared his throat and looked down now at his desk. "Well. That's not exactly the way he put it. He said he *thought* the book would sell. He thought, given the controversy about lowering the voting age and the driving age and all the rest, well, that he could market it. He could market you."

It wasn't like Clayton at all to talk about "marketing." He was all about "craft" and "literary merit." "And you think I should do this?"

He turned in his seat so he was looking out the window for a second and then he quickly turned back. "Nigel, I have one book of poetry in print. Maybe five hundred people in the entire world have read it. And it wasn't that good. I've written three novels and none of them have found publishers. I've known Bill since high school. He's not a big fan of literature with a capital 'L' but he does know how to make a book successful. It's the chance of a lifetime."

And that was yet another point of no return.

"But I have to finish it first, right?"

"No. You have to sign the contract, accept the advance, and then finish it by the deadline."

"What kind of deadline?"

He smiled. "Same deadline as you always had. Finish it by the last week of school. If Bill's not totally bullshitting me, he could have it out in paperback within a month after that. This is not 'normal' publishing. But he's afraid someone else will move in on this turf. There are non-fiction authors already on it. But nobody has nailed down a novel quite like yours—especially a sixteen-year-old kid."

Chapter Eleven

When I called Michelle to tell her my news, she said I should come right over to see her. But I said I didn't want to share this right now with Franklin and Mary. Just her, Michelle.

"Don't worry about them," she said.

"Are you feeling any better?" I asked.

"Much."

"Then meet me at the coffee shop, okay?"

"Sure."

I arrived before her and sat at a corner table. When she walked in, she looked transformed. Radiant. I couldn't take my eyes off her as she walked across the room. As soon as she sat down, before she had a chance to speak, I kissed her hard on the mouth as everyone around us watched. She didn't pull away but leaned forward and put her heart and soul into that kiss.

"I'm going to have my novel published," I told her.

Her eyes brightened. She looked so much healthier. "Fantastic. I knew it was good." She seemed happy, ecstatic even. But something was odd. She didn't seem surprised.

I tried to ignore that and told her all that Clayton had to say.

"You can do it," she said. "I have faith in you."

I shook my head in uncertainty. I was ready to admit what I had felt after I had walked out of Clayton's classroom, after the initial thrill wore off. "Yeah, but I'm not sure I have faith in me."

"Just write it. Write the story. Follow Austin, Krieg, and Tamara. Let Austin write the story. It's his life." She said this just as if they were real people.

"Austin's a bit confused. He says so himself."

"Austin's Austin. But hey, he's got a girlfriend. And he's getting laid."

I think I blushed then. The way she said it. "But a guy his age with an older girl. Is that a bit odd?"

"He was fifteen and she was seventeen. Two years difference. Then she turns eighteen and soon he'll be sixteen. Still two years difference. They're still who they are."

"But in the scene I finished, he's still fifteen and she's

eighteen. Why did I write it that way?"

"It's just numbers. Isn't that part of what your novel is about—how we judge people by the number assigned to their age and how different the world could be if we started to break down some of those barriers?"

She sounded a little too teacher-like then. Like something Clayton would have said. Like she knew more about my novel than I did. I was still filled with those self doubts that had crept in after the flush of glory at believing my book would be published.

"You do realize I'm five months older than you," she said, smiling now.

"Does this mean you are going to seduce me like Tamara seduced Austin?"

She fluttered her eyelashes and I couldn't help but notice how dark and beautiful her eyes were. I reached out and held her hands and noticed that she wasn't wearing the metal bracelet. "How do you know it was she who seduced him? I didn't say that in the manuscript."

She paused and then said, "Because she's older. Besides, sometimes guys who are uncertain about themselves have to be coached."

"Coached?" I asked.

"Yes."

Over the next few weeks, I pretty much ignored most of my other school work and put all my effort into the novel. I decided not to allow Uncle Franklin to post any more of it on-line, though. He called me up to protest and pleaded for me to continue, but I held my ground. I thought that if it was all up there for anyone to read, who would buy the book?

"That's probably shrewd of you," Franklin said. "They'll just have to wait for the release." I was surprised that he gave up so quickly.

I gave a couple more chapters to Clayton who turned them over to Botzweiler and then I received a quick e-mail note from Botzweiler's secretary: *William would like to have a video conference with you on Thursday at 4 P.M. your time. He's on business in London but wants to talk to you right away.*

I said I could do that.

On Thursday at 4 P.M. I sat down at my computer in my bedroom and waited. Then Botzweiler appeared on my screen. He wore glasses and was nearly bald, but had a pony tail that hung down behind him. He was staring right at me and his eyes were intense. He was a little intimidating. So this was what a publisher looked like.

I adjusted my video-cam and waited for him to speak first.

"Good afternoon, Nigel. How are you?"

"Fine. How are things in London?"

"Crowded. Busy. A little warm. But I like it here."

"I've never been to England."

"That could change," he said. "So let's get right to the point."

"Sure, let's do that," I said.

"This novel of yours that you are writing for Tom Clayton's class—it's good."

"Thanks."

"I don't think it's great, mind you. Don't get a swelled head over it or anything. I just think you've tapped into something. I see it on the streets here in the U.K. I see it in the States and in Canada."

"I'm not sure I know exactly what you mean."

"I call it 'the end of adolescence' movement but you don't hear anyone else saying it that way. They call it youth rights or age discrimination. It takes many forms. Kids want to vote younger, drink younger, drive younger. They want the old rules taken away. They want a level playing field."

"But my novel isn't advocating any of that. It's just set in the future when—"

He waved his hand and cut me off. "I know all that. I've read what you've written so far. I like the way you are still telling a story—and a difficult one at that. It's not utopia. But it's a vision of the future."

"I don't know how it will end."

"But you can finish it, right?"

"Yes."

"Good. Because, here's the thing. The shrinks and political writers are writing books about the movement but no one has tapped into the real heart of it. No young writer has given it a voice."

"And you think my novel somehow does just that?"

Botzweiler stroked his jaw and then, with his other hand, ran it over his head like he was smoothing down his hair, although he didn't have any hair—on top, at least. "Well, maybe yes and maybe no. But your vision is compelling. And controversial. I mean, a world—or at least parts of the world—run by teenagers. Wow."

"Fifteen to twenty-one," I corrected. "Older teens and young adults."

"Sure. Oh, don't think I don't get it." He seemed quite animated now. "My generation was going to change the world. We had a revolution planned. We already thought we were halfway there."

"And what happened?"

He tapped his bald head and smiled. "We grew up. We got old. We sold out. I started out publishing books about growing your own organic food, living off the power grid, and alternatives to the traditional mom and pop family, and now I'm publishing bestsellers about the sex lives of pop stars."

I wasn't sure why he was telling me this. Right then, I wasn't sure I liked this guy. Or trusted him. "There's not much sex in my novel."

"I'm okay with that. I want to publish your book because I think people need to read your story. They need to see your vision."

"It's not really a vision. It's just a kind of fantasy. A what-if kind of thing."

"Right. About a future where kids take charge and adults retire at twenty-one. About an alternative to wars and social injustice."

"An imperfect world."

"It will always be an imperfect world."

I said nothing but looked away from the screen for a minute and out the window of my bedroom—at a bird sitting on the branch of the tree there. One small black grackle. I'd seen him there often and wondered why he hovered outside my bedroom window.

"Mr. Clayton says you think my book will make a lot of money."

"It could. No promises."

"Is that why you want to publish it?"

"Partly. I'm a businessman, you know. I have to admit to that. I don't eat granola and goat's cheese and live in a tree house. But I also like to make things happen. When I'm not publishing trash about rock stars, I try to balance things by publishing good books. Important books. But they only become important if they are marketed properly. Because you are sixteen and because you've written this book, I believe we can market you."

I didn't like the sound of that at all. Botzweiler saw the face I gave him.

"I know. Makes you feel like a Barbie doll? This marketing thing?"

"It does."

Botzweiler seemed to be checking his watch. "I saw the postings on the Internet. Now I know you didn't make any money from that, but what was that all about? Why was it there?"

"It wasn't exactly my idea."

"But you got a lot of hits. You engendered a hell of a lot of interest. You stirred up something. I don't suppose you received any fan mail."

"Some." Actually there had been a ridiculous amount. I don't even know how they all found my e-mail address. "But I had my detractors as well."

Botzweiler smiled. "Controversy is good for an author. It sells books. So do we have a deal?"

What deal, I wondered. He hadn't mentioned any terms, or any amount of money. I felt bewildered. I felt like I was about to merchandise my soul. He noticed my hesitancy.

"Look, Nigel. This is a chance of a lifetime. I have faith in you and you haven't even finished the book. No publisher would take a leap like this. I will. I believe in you."

"Why?" I asked.

"Because Tom Clayton says you can do this. He believes in you. I trust him and I trust my own instinct."

"What if it bombs? What if nobody buys it?"

"Wouldn't be the first time I was wrong. But what if it finds its mark?"

It's funny. That's what scared me the most. I really didn't have any great dream to be a spokesman for any cause. I wasn't sure I even wanted this.

"In two days, you'll receive a contract sent by courier. Take a look at it. Get some advice if you like. You'll like what you see." He looked at his watch again. "Gotta go. My number will be on the paperwork. Call me anytime on my cell. I'll be in Frankfurt tomorrow."

And he blipped off my screen. I switched off my video-cam and put my computer on standby. The grackle was still on the branch of the tree watching me and I walked to the window. The world of my front yard—birds, trees, grass, and flowers—seemed peaceful. I thought of my father and me planting those cherry trees in front of the school. I wasn't sure I wanted any of it to change.

Chapter Twelve

When Austin turned sixteen, he moved in with Tamara in her apartment by the sea. A month later, a raging storm, unlike anything that had hit those shores for fifty years, swept over the coastline. The waves were huge and the sea levels surged higher than anyone could remember. The parking lot and first floor of the building were flooded. Austin and Tamara remained in the dark apartment, twelve stories up, and rode it out through the night. They were both scared, but in the morning they were unharmed.

"We're still being punished for the bad decisions from the past," Tamara said. "Even back in the 1980s, they knew they had made some monumentally bad decisions—and had allowed old ways to continue way too long. The climate changes were already happening. There was so little effort to make a difference."

"Do you think anything we are doing now can help?"

"Yes," she said. "But we still need to get the other countries on board. Remember the old locomotive analogy? I think we have almost stopped the train. Now we have to get it moving in the other direction."

Tamara was three years from retirement. After that she'd do volunteer work for sure, but the real jobs would be taken over by younger people. She had helped Austin become more confident. They were good for each other.

Austin now had a full client load of twenty-five serious offenders. For a while, he thought the weight of their crimes and their grief was going to smother him. He started to see a counselor himself—a fifteen-year-old who was new to the job. Austin was startled to see how confident and bright the kid was. He had been prepared well.

And then, after what seemed like three months of severe

depression that had come in the wake of what seemed to be real improvement, Jonathan Krieg broke down during a session with Austin. He cried long and loud and he asked Austin to help him save his own life.

And Austin did that. He tapped a code into the computer and sat Jonathan down at the workstation.

"What is it?" Krieg asked.

"Unlimited access to all the pain control research that's taken place since you've been incarcerated."

"But I don't think I can go there. Not now. Not after taking some-one's life."

"People know about your research. You'll have something to offer."

"But everything has moved on. Besides, I'm too old."

"In a few years I'll be too old, too. Too old to be employed, to be in charge. But not too old to offer whatever I can give. You're never too old for that. If you have something worthwhile to offer, someone will listen. Age won't matter."

Krieg clicked onto a site and began to read what was on the screen. "This is all totally new. I don't even understand the terms."

"You'll figure it out."

Austin reached over and typed Krieg's full name into the search window and was directed to dozens of pages of information. "Some people are still discussing your ideas. A lot of research continued where you left off. I'm sure some of those researchers would love to hear from you."

"But they'd all know, right?"

"Know that you killed your colleague? Yes, probably."

"And what would they think?"

"I don't know. But maybe you are ready to find out."

Michelle never finished her own novel. Neither did more than two-thirds of Clayton's class. Tom Clayton knew that he'd probably not be able to offer creative writing again—at least not to a class with such high expectations. But I finished *Future Prime*. Michelle and Mr. Clayton were the only ones to read it. And

William Botzweiler, of course. I still wasn't sure about the ending. And at that point, I didn't have a clue as to what would happen next. I was a little scared but scared of all the wrong things.

I had started reading more about the youth movement. It seemed to be strongest in the U.K. and in Canada, with pockets of intensity in the northeast U.S. and the west coast of the U.S. as well. Some of the fringe elements were pretty damn weird: some teens wanting to be allowed to be in the military as young as thirteen, some wanting the right to marry and have children at that age as well. There were proposals for radical new schools where students were paid to attend and could live on their own. Demands from some young people to be trained for high-paying jobs at an early age and legislation to prevent "age discrimination" down to age fourteen, if not lower.

I made a point of trying not to let any of that influence what I was writing. But I had signed Botzweiler's generous contract. And I knew that when the book was released, the media would fit it into what was going on out there. The publisher would see to that.

Clayton gave me an A+. He offered some suggestions for improving the manuscript before I sent it out and they were all bang on. *Future Prime* ends when Austin turns twenty-one and he begins the next phase of his life—his adult life.

Michelle had been acting strangely during that last month of school. I had ignored her, perhaps. I was obsessed with my story, living in the strange fantasy world of the future. She was always positive and supportive but I had inadvertently pushed her away. She was sick for the entire final week of school and I went to see her every day, but it wasn't until Friday that Franklin and Mary would let me in to visit.

She was still in bed, pale and tired-looking. Sick. Very sick. "I'm okay," she said. "This is nothing new. For the past few years, I've had these spells. They knock me out for about a week at a time. And then I get better."

"What is it?"

"It has a long, weird name. I'd rather not say it out loud. Just naming it makes me feel worse. I'll be okay, though." And then she dropped the bombshell. "I'm going to have to go back home in a couple of weeks. The specialist is back there."

"Back in California?"

She blinked. "Yes. I need to go home."

I felt the blood drain out of my face. She had never really spoken about going back home. I leaned forward and brushed my hand along her face. It felt very warm. "How come you never spoke about it?"

"Because it would make me too sad, I guess. I didn't want to think about having to leave you."

"Then don't leave. Stay here." I was thinking I'd do anything to keep her. I felt a pain in my chest.

"Franklin and Mary will be leaving, too. This isn't really their home either."

I was thinking about my book then, about the contract and the money. "I can rent an apartment. You can move in with me. I already received the advance on the novel. It's more than enough."

She smiled and sat up a little straighter. "Wow," was all she could say.

"We can travel to California whenever you want if you need to see your doctor and your parents. I promise."

"I can't," she said. "It's not that easy. I wish I could."

"Michelle, I was really nothing before you came into my life. This whole book thing happened because you believed in me. I couldn't have done it without you."

"Thank you for saying that. But yes, you could have. I know that for a fact."

"How could you know?"

"I just know. You have to believe me."

I looked at the metal bracelet she was again wearing. I looked at the strange symbols on it. She had stopped wearing it at school and in public but she had it on here in her own bedroom.

Her mysteries had always attracted me, but right then I was feeling lost and more than a little hurt. "You mean you can just leave here, leave me, and move back home?"

"I have no choice."

"You know how much that is going to hurt?"

"I guess I do now."

"I was thinking that when this book comes out and if I have to be out there in the public doing whatever, it will scare the shit out of me. I couldn't do it—but then I thought of you being there with me and I realized I could handle it. If you were there."

"I'm sorry. I can't do that."

I let the silence settle in—cold and fearful. "Then I'll come visit you." I paused. "No, I'll do better than that. I'll move to California so I can be near you."

She looked devastated now. I saw the tears well up in her eyes. "I'm sorry. You can't do that."

"Why not?" I asked.

But she just began to cry and slid back down in the bed and covered her head with the blanket.

I was angry. I couldn't understand why something was being given to me and something so important was about to be taken away at the same time. I was beginning to wish that

Michelle had never come into my life, that I had never taken Clayton's class. I wanted everything to go back to being normal. Life may have been dull, but it did not have this pain I was feeling now. For a fleeting moment, I thought of my home and my parents—but then I realized I had moved on from finding any comfort in all that. Michelle was my world now.

I walked out of her room and went downstairs. Franklin and Mary were in the kitchen talking. I burst in and addressed Franklin, my voice shaking. "Why don't you tell me the truth?"

Franklin blinked and gave me one of his goofy half-smiles. "The truth about what?" He seemed calm but Mary seemed like something was bothering her. She wouldn't look directly at me.

"What's wrong with Michelle?" I demanded.

"She's never hidden from you the fact that she gets ill often."

"So what is it that's wrong with her?"

"It's a neurological disorder," Mary said. "It comes and goes."

I looked at them. They could not look straight back at me. I had the feeling they were lying. Covering something up.

"But if she's so sick, why is she here? Why did she move here and why are you here with her?"

"Mary and I had rented this house," Franklin began, "and Michelle's parents thought she needed to get away for a time. Things weren't going well at her school, so we offered to help out. At first she was to stay for just a couple of weeks, but then she met you."

"But she has to return for treatment now," Mary added. "She's been away longer than planned."

"But why can't I go to be with her? She says I can't, but nobody can stop me."

Michelle came into the kitchen then and sat down. She looked at me and then at her aunt and uncle. "I want to stay," she said.

"You can't," Mary insisted.

"I don't think the book will get published if I leave now," Michelle said, looking at Mary and then at Franklin.

"What does the book have to do with it?" I asked. "I don't really care about the stupid novel. Not now. I care about you."

"I know. And that's why you need to let them publish the book. And I want to be here when it happens."

And then Franklin said a very strange thing. "I guess we don't have a choice."

Chapter Thirteen

Michelle's health seemed to improve after that. Whenever I asked her about the "neurological disorder," she'd refuse to talk about it. One day, sitting with her in the public library, the two of us reading, I asked her to find a medical book and tell me more about what her illness was. She refused.

"In Erewhon, they thought it was bad luck to talk about anyone's health," she answered, evading my question.

"Where's Erewhon?"

"It's Nowhere, spelled backwards ... or almost backwards. It's an imaginary place created by Samuel Butler in the nineteenth century. The people there had gods with names like Truth and

Justice, Strength, Hope, and Fear. Each is in charge of the thing they are named for. And they each have their own set of laws. The gods Time and Space, for example, insist that no two objects can occupy the same physical location at the same time."

"Seems reasonable. But what about sex?"

She smiled. "Maybe they make an exception for that. I don't know."

I brushed her hair lightly with my fingers. It had been a while since the subject of sex had been brought up. Michelle and I had grown more physical with each other but we had never had sex. She seemed so fragile sometimes.

"In Erewhon there had once been a race of people who knew perfectly what the future would be. It was said they all died, out of the misery that came from knowing the future."

"I could see that," I said. "If we all knew exactly how difficult some things in our lives were going to be—if we could see it in front of us clearly—some of us might not be able to handle it."

"Could you?" she asked.

"Yes," I said. And then I paused. "As long as I had you there with me."

She leaned forward and kissed me. My book fell to the floor with a thud and people looked at us.

"Do you think it's bad luck that I wrote about the future?

That both of us wrote about it?"

"No. Most people are afraid to look into the future. They're like the people of Erewhon. They see the future as a dark hallway ahead. And the light is so bright right where we are in the here and now that we can't see where we are going. We can only perceive the present. Some people prefer to walk backwards into the future, not looking at the dark at all, but watching the past as it fades away."

"You read too many books," I said. "Let's get out of here."

We took a long walk after that down by the harbor. The waves lapped against the walkway and some sailboats cruised along on the blue water. We walked until Michelle became tired and I had to find a cab to take her back home. In the back of the taxi, she kissed me again. But this time I felt sadness in her kiss.

And then *Future Prime* appeared in print. Botzweiler had not lied. He was good at what he did. Almost a month from the day school was over, a box arrived with my copies of the first printing. It had a striking cover and it somehow didn't seem real. I had a hard time getting my head around the reality that this was *my* book. Within a week it was in the stores. The e-mails started to trickle in. And then more.

I didn't get my first truly threatening e-mail until the book had been out for two weeks. And it wasn't my last. I didn't tell my parents. They didn't know what to make of the fact that their son had actually published a book and that people were reading it. It came out simultaneously in the U.S., the U.K., and Canada.

I had heard from Jeanne Piercey, the publicist of Twin Bridges, that they had some sort of tour planned for me. I didn't know if I was ready for that. I had my first interview with a lady journalist from the *Daily News* who I don't think had read the book. But it gave me a clue as to what was ahead.

Why did you write the book? Why do you think the future will be like this? Why would adults turn over the reins of society to teenagers? Where did you get these ideas from?

My answers were all pretty vague. It's a novel, I kept saying. It's something I made up out of my head. It's not real.

Gary caught up with me one day at the coffee shop and asked me to sign his copy of the book. "You nailed it, dude. This book is going to light the spark. Thanks for doing this, man." He had stopped being aggressive. He acted like he was my best friend.

When I read the article in the *Daily News*, I didn't understand it at first. It had little to do with anything I had said.

Local teen writer, Nigel Lukes, has penned what might be the most controversial book of the year. In it he proposes a radical restructuring of society where teens rule and adults have few if

any rights and responsibilities. He seems to be adding fuel pur-
posefully to the fire of the worldwide youth rights movement
that has seen demonstrations in major cities in North America,
Europe, and Australia.

Lukes' story is a disturbing view of what the author seems to
think is a utopian future and he is advocating that only young
people will be able to undo the harm done by generations of
adults who have been responsible for war and the ravages to
the environment.

And then she quoted a local church leader, Reverend Luther
Oswald, who said:

I haven't read the book, nor will I ever. And I urge every parent
to ensure that their sons and daughters never pick up a copy of
it. It is a malicious book that will attract weak, youthful minds to
think about ideas that could do great harm to us all, should
anyone take this filth seriously.

When I finished reading that, I couldn't believe it. Was Oswald
talking about *my* book? It was just a story, a story I'd written
for a high school creative writing class. What the hell was he
talking about?

The first review I read was from a rather left-leaning online magazine called *Rabble*. I had a hard time accepting that words like "brilliant" and "prophetic" were being used to describe me and my book. My publicist told me to set a Google Alert for the title of the book and for my name, and before long I was discovering that the book was being talked about far and wide. And not all of what was said was good. Not by a long shot.

The novel shocked and appalled many. What I had written was threatening to many people. "Dangerous" was the word that started appearing on a regular basis. My parents were tuning in to what was going on. How could they not? All their friends were talking to them about their son. I was either a boy wonder or the Antichrist. Nobody seemed to be sitting on the fence. And what came up over and over was that those who had nasty things to say about me had, in most cases, never read the book. Someone told my dad that another local minister had talked about my book in his Sunday sermon, urging parents to throw it in the trash or burn it if they saw their kids reading it.

Mr. Clayton showed up at my house one day and asked to talk. He looked worried. "Nigel, I'm not sure about what I got you into. I had no idea this would happen."

At that point, I was a bit stunned by it all—the good stuff

and the bad—but I figured my five minutes of fame would blow over pretty soon.

"No one pays much attention to a first novel. This is unheard of," Clayton said.

"What should I do?"

He rubbed his hands together and then put them down on the table. "Nothing," he said. "Try to be invisible."

I'd already seen my picture posted on dozens of Web sites. I'd been on local TV and in the papers. "I am kind of freaked out by all the attention," I said. "I'm ready to go back to being a kid."

"Good plan. But you've got a problem."

"I do?"

"For sure. My old buddy William B. called to say he has some big promotion plans for you. It's called the book tour."

"Yeah, the publicist keeps referring to it, but she never quite tells me what it involves."

"Well, my book tour was giving readings to audiences of three in public libraries in the boonies. I don't think that's what they have in mind for you."

"What should I do?"

"I don't know. I've been following the press on this. Your book has really hit a nerve. Some people are excited by it, some appalled."

"So I've noticed. Um … is it really *that* good?"

He put his hands up in the air. "I wouldn't say this before to you but, well, no, it's not that great."

"But you gave me an A."

"Right. For a high school kid writing his first novel, a novel that had some stimulating ideas in it, it was damn good. You deserved the A. And I got carried away suggesting you might get it published. But it's not as good as they say and it is not as dangerous, either."

"Oh," I said, feeling a little deflated. But then Tom Clayton was himself a writer. Heck, maybe he was just jealous. I was feeling a tad defensive. I had already begun to learn to ignore the critics and glom onto the ones who called the book "visionary" and "ground-breaking."

"Botzweiler's gonna talk to you. I don't know what he has planned. But you don't have to do as he says. Too much success at a young age can kill you. Look at Jim Morrison, Jimi Hendrix, Janis Joplin."

"Who?" I asked.

"Never mind. Just remember that you are in charge of your life. You decide, not Botzweiler or anyone else."

My parents sat me down for my third major lecture concerning my book, my future, and the fact I had not consulted with them on all this. They had not even read the book until it came out. They didn't understand what all the fuss was about—didn't think the book was any big deal—but there was a fuss and that's what worried them.

"Can't you just tell the publisher to take it off the market?" my mom asked.

"I don't think it works that way. Besides it's selling great."

"But we're worried about all this publicity," my dad said. "It's not always a good thing to be in the limelight, especially over anything that is controversial."

"It's just a novel," I said. "It's not a prediction. And none of it is real."

"But where did you ever come up with those ideas?" my mom asked. She was a pretty practical, down-to-earth person.

"Well, it was just from my imagination. I'd write a chapter and let Michelle read it and she'd encourage me to keep going. I probably wouldn't have been able to finish it if it wasn't for her."

"Way to go, Michelle," my dad said cynically.

I guess I knew all along that Michelle *had* been the inspiration that kept me going. I mean, the course was one thing, but I could have just gone through the motions, given up at my usual 176 pages, or written a novel about hockey, like Dave Greer. But it was Michelle who had brought out the best in me. What was the term? She had been my *muse*.

That same afternoon, the publicist called and asked me to go to my computer for another video conference with Mr. Botzweiler. Most contact with the publishing house was e-mail or over the phone, but Botzweiler always wanted the face-to-face video conferences from wherever he was. I hung up and went to my computer. A pop-up alerted me to the fact he was on-line. He didn't even say hello.

"We're into the second printing," William Botzweiler announced.

"Is that good?"

"It's great." He was smiling ear to ear. "Aren't you pleased?"

"I'm not so sure," I said.

He laughed. "Hey, wait till you see your royalty check."

"Mr. Clayton had told me not to get my hopes up."

"Clayton doesn't understand much about publishing."

"He came by a while ago."

Botzweiler looked puzzled. "What did he have to say?"

"He congratulated me," I lied, "and told me about what it would be like to do readings at public libraries. Sounds like fun."

"Forget the public library circuit. You're not quite right for blue-haired ladies in tennis shoes."

"Darn," I said, trying to keep things light.

"We've got some big things planned for you."

I was hoping he wouldn't say that. "Really?"

"Really." William B. was polishing the top of his bald head again, checking to see if any hair had grown back in. "Radio and TV talk shows, podcasts, a couple of university lectures. There's a ton of interest. It's exciting."

I felt a kind of panic setting in.

"We've put out a few feelers. There *really* is a lot of interest. Everyone wants you."

"I don't think I can," I said. "I'm not ready for this." I was thinking of what Clayton had said. I was thinking of what my parents had said.

Botzweiler scowled. "Nigel, I understand that it seems a bit much because you are new at it, but Jeanne will coach you. You'll be a natural."

"But what about all those people out there who hate my guts? I've stopped reading my e-mails and I stopped reading all the reviews and opinions, good and bad. It's just a little too weird."

"Do you know how good *bad* publicity is? The more rotten things people say about you or your book the more it sells. And it's all bullshit anyway. They don't know what they're talking about. The world is filled with opinionated assholes."

"But I don't understand what is so shocking in the book.

What are they afraid of?"

"Change, Nigel. They're afraid of change. You think you're the only one getting nasty e-mails. But it's all just farting in the wind. You are the poster boy for freedom of speech and freedom of the press. The critics think censorship is the answer. And that would put us back into the Dark Ages."

I wondered how much William B. actually knew about the Dark Ages. I sure didn't know much.

"I'm sorry," I said, trying to hold my ground. "I really don't think I can do it."

He gave me a hard look. And I mean *hard*. I wished just then that we didn't have video-cams. I wished he was just a disembodied voice on the other end of the phone. Damn. You could tell he wasn't the slightest bit used to hearing someone disagree with his wishes. He took a deep breath. "Just think about it, Nigel. I'll have Jeanne get back to you with the details. You can start close to home and work outward from there."

"I don't think so," I said again.

His voice changed a bit and his expression got harder. "It's in the contract, Nigel. Just take a look. You signed it. And it's a legal agreement. In it, you've already agreed to the book tour."

Chapter Fourteen

Two days later, the publicist, Jeanine Piercey, called but I didn't pick up the phone. I let her leave a message. I needed more time to think. I really had stopped reading my e-mails and alerts to blogs and articles about me posted on the Internet. I was feeling edgy and uncertain and truly wished I hadn't gotten myself into this. I wasn't prepared to go out into the world like some whiz kid guru to be idolized or to have rocks thrown at me. Nobody had told me that writing a book could make life so much more complicated.

I asked Michelle to meet me down by the harbor. She was sitting on a bench by the water when I arrived and she didn't

---

see me as I approached. I stopped in my tracks and just looked at her, realizing just how much I needed her right now.

I walked up to her and, as she looked up, I bent over and kissed her. As I did, I realized she'd been crying.

"What's wrong?" I asked.

"I don't know what to do," she said. "I'm so confused."

I didn't understand. I thought it was me who was confused. "Tell me about it."

"I can't and I wish I could. I may have made a mistake."

I was baffled. "What do you mean?"

"Moving here. Meeting you. And then losing you."

"You haven't lost me." I was thinking about the book tour, wondering how she knew anything about it. She was still crying. There were some pieces of this puzzle I was missing.

"I came here 'cause of you," she said. "I knew who you were."

"How could that be?"

"I can't explain."

"But you knew we would meet if you moved here? You knew I'd be attracted to you and that we'd be together?"

"I thought it was possible. I didn't know for sure."

"What about the whole illness thing?"

"Oh, I wish I had made that up, but I didn't."

I sat down and stared across the water at a ferry headed our way from across the harbor. "What if we just got on that ferry when it gets in? What if we take it to the other side and then just get off and leave? Go somewhere together."

"Run away. Just like that?"

"Yes. Just like that."

She shook her head. "That's not what is going to happen." There was certainty in her voice. "Franklin and Mary think I need quiet and rest. They want to take me to a cabin they have rented in the mountains north of here. A retreat, they call it. They found it on the Internet."

"And you need to do this to get better?"

"Yes. If I'm going to continue, I need it." She paused. If she left, I feared I might never see her again. "But they want you to come, too."

"Really?" The world suddenly seemed brighter.

"Will you?"

This didn't require any thinking whatsoever. "Yes. When do we leave?"

"This afternoon," she said.

"Wow! Soon," was all I could muster. This change of events seemed very, very odd but I was afraid to question it. All I knew was that I would get to be with Michelle. It didn't matter wherever the hell we were going with crazy Uncle Frank and Aunt Mary. If Michelle was going, so was I. To hell with William Botzweiler and his freaking contact.

As soon as I walked in the door, my mother told me about four more phone calls from the publisher and one from an angry parent who screamed at her for letting her son write "that book." My mom looked frazzled and distressed.

"I'm sorry I caused you this trouble, Mom. I didn't know."

"Who could have guessed?" she said.

And then I explained about going away for a few days with Michelle to a retreat in the mountains.

She looked a little confused. Heck, I was confused. But I had to be with Michelle and I didn't want to deal with the publishing world right now. "I'll call your father and talk it over with him."

"Sure." I went to my room to pack. One way or the other, I'd make them see the importance of doing this.

My mom and I ate a quiet lunch together and I felt like a little kid again. I missed that feeling. How was it that I had grown up so quickly? I wondered. One day, you're sitting in your room, coloring with crayons, with nothing to worry about, and the next you're feeling like the world has heaped way too much responsibility on you. And you're grown up. No turning back.

"Your father said you can go if I think it's the right thing."

"And what did you say?"

"I said I trusted you. I said I wanted you to avoid getting

caught up in all of this publicity, so going away might be a good thing. And I like Michelle. She isn't like other girls your age. She's quiet and thoughtful."

"I hadn't really thought about it that way. But you're right. She's not like any other girl I ever met. I'm afraid I'm going to lose her."

"That would be sad," was all my mom said. "But you're still young." Which I guess meant: you're still young and some-one else would come along. It didn't feel that way.

Franklin was driving and Mary sat beside him. I hugged my mom and got in the back seat of the car with Michelle.

"I feel like we *are* running away," I said.

"We are." She smiled a little-girl smile, but I suddenly wondered what I was doing. Was I really ready for this? No, I probably wasn't. But at the same time, something in me was urging me to move forward into this unknown territory.

Mary was humming some song I didn't recognize and Franklin was wearing an earpiece, listening to something. It made him seem like he was in another world. "It's a GPS system. He's getting directions. Uncle Frank wouldn't know how to find his way to the corner store without GPS."

Uncle Frank was also about the oddest driver I had ever observed. He seemed to be looking more at the windshield instead of the traffic ahead. He talked out loud about the driving. "Stop on Red. Go on Green," he said. "Speed up on Yellow. Right hand turn onto the 103. Watch for the Wal-Mart on the left."

Michelle and I sat quietly in the back seat. I held her hand the whole way and felt very shy. The city gave way to strip malls and then an industrial park and finally empty spaces and forests. I could see the mountains ahead, almost like dark clouds on the horizon.

"Does California look like this?" I asked.

"Not anymore," she said wistfully.

Franklin continued to receive instructions as we drove. "Turn left by the stream onto a gravel road," he repeated out loud. And he turned.

After a three-hour drive, we stopped in front of a beautiful two-story log cabin with big cathedral windows. A noisy stream ran beside the cabin. The trees themselves were tall pines and the ground was covered in a carpet of brown pine needles. The smell was incredible. As soon as we got out of the car, we all simultaneously took a deep breath.

"And now we leave the rest of the world behind," Mary said.

I half expected Franklin to open the trunk and lift a case of beer out. But it wasn't going to be like that. "Ever meditate, Nigel?" he asked.

"I tried it but I'm not good at it. Too many thoughts going through my head."

"Of course," he said. "But it's good for you." He seemed like a different person altogether now. Much more serious. Mary seemed the same way. Both somehow transformed. Both acting as if they'd dropped some comic personas that they'd previously taken on just for my sake. "Meditation has been helpful to Michelle. I think it's helped slow the progress of her condition."

"It has, Uncle Franklin," she said. "I'm sure it has." She addressed them differently now, more formal in tone.

"Would you let us teach you some meditation techniques?" Mary asked me.

"You can try," I answered, suddenly wondering who these people were and what exactly was going on here. Michelle saw my doubts and squeezed my hand.

The door was not locked. We walked in and Mary asked Michelle and me to follow her. "This is the meditation room," Mary said, opening the wooden door to a large room with polished log walls, no furniture, and mats on the floor that reminded me of wrestling. Then she led us up the stairway and opened a door and said to us, "And this will be your room." She meant for both Michelle and me. If I had had any second thoughts up to that moment, they all vanished instantly.

Michelle and I went for a walk in the woods after that and I felt more peaceful than I had ever felt in my life. "Everything moves too fast, doesn't it?" I said.

"Yes. But every once in a while, like right now, you wish that you could make time stop. Really stop. That's partly what this is about," Michelle said. "The world moves on without us. As it always does. And we retreat."

"It's all so beautiful. I've forgotten how cut off I've felt from nature since I was a kid. I just didn't think it was this important. This powerful." I was listening to the sound of water sliding over the rocks in the stream, watching the sunlight filter down through the pine branches. And I remembered that spring day, planting those cherry trees with my father.

"I'm going to tell you some things while we're here that you're going to find hard to accept. You're going to have to keep a very open mind."

"Oh boy," was all I could say. I had no idea what she was talking about. But this all sounded very weird. Scary, even.

"I guess I'm asking you to trust me on this."

I swallowed hard. "I trust you."

When we returned to the house, Franklin and Mary had prepared a meal for us. "Pure vegetarian," Mary said. "I hope you like it."

It was very good and very different. "A couple of old Asian recipes my grandfather taught me. It's amazing what you can do with tofu, dried seaweed, and the right spices," Franklin said.

After dinner, Michelle and I went back to our room, talked, and went to bed together. We held each other through the night. Sometimes I awoke and just put my face close to hers and listened to her breathe.

Franklin tapped on the door at about six in the morning. "You guys care to join us in the meditation room?"

Michelle waited for me to answer. I was wishing I didn't have to get out of bed. I felt like staying there with her forever, but I said, "Sure. We'll be right down."

"Remember," Michelle said. "Keep an open mind."

Mary and Frank had on what looked like judo robes to me. They seemed older to me now, but more peaceful. Both were stretching, doing what I guessed to be Tai Chi moves.

I followed Michelle's lead and sat down on the mat. "Are you ready?" she asked.

I nodded. "Ready." Part of me was thinking I was about to be brainwashed, turned into a zombie, have crazy instructions imprinted in my head. I don't know what else. But I guess I just wasn't familiar with any of this.

"Close your eyes," Franklin said. "Reflect on something you are not happy with in your life."

I couldn't help but think about the book I had unleashed and about the fact that someday all too soon Michelle would move back home and I might lose her forever.

"Breathe in deeply and then let it go. When you breathe in, focus on the unhappiness, but when you breathe out, just let it go. Do this over and over."

I felt myself relaxing and moving into a dreamy place, not unlike sleep but still feeling awake. I kept my eyes closed and breathed.

"Now I want you to think about death and dying. Breathe in the idea of your own death and then breathe out, accepting that your death will come and it will be the most natural thing in the world."

That was a bit much, but I tried to stay focused on the possibility of dying. When you are young, you don't think you will ever die. Against all logic, I expected to live forever.

"The Tibetans taught that our fear of death is based on fears of losing the body and of what it may be like going through the death experience. If you can accept that you are your awareness, not your body, you'll have an easier time letting go of the body when the time comes. Continue to breathe in all your fears of death and exhale your acceptance of death. And then focus on your awareness of being alive. After you die, that awareness will still be there but your experiences will be different."

In the dark internal place where I had gone, his words made perfect sense. I had not really thought about these things but his words rang perfectly clear to me. I was shocked. And I realized that this, too, was part of my "awareness."

"Now be very still. Slow your breathing. Imagine that your senses are enhanced and you can feel the life force of others. You can feel happiness and sadness of people you know and of strangers, too. At first it will feel overwhelming, but accept it. Let it wash over you."

I sensed some small hint of what he was saying, perhaps real or perhaps imagined. But it was overwhelming and I almost opened my eyes. I felt panic replacing the peace.

"Slow your breathing back down. Focus on the breath."

I did and I calmed.

"Be aware now of all the people in your life. Imagine a clear, sparkling light flowing through you that you want to share with them all. Imagine all those in the world who are being born and dying right now. Picture yourself sharing joy and happiness with them all.

"Now you see a clear light coming towards you. Move into it and continue to breathe. Stay there in the light as long as you can."

I went somewhere. I'm not sure where. And I must have

stayed there for minutes or maybe much longer. I seemed to have lost all sense of time.

When I awoke, I was alone in the room with Franklin. He was staring straight at me. But Michelle was gone.

Chapter Fifteen

"It's okay," Franklin said. "She just had to take a break. You should go up in a minute. What did you think about the meditation exercise?"

"Powerful stuff," I said. "Where does it come from?"

"It's Tibetan. Something taught to me when I was quite young. It's a different way of looking at the world. There are many such exercises and meditations. It's not everybody's cup of tea, but I find it helps you accept some of the inevitable changes that happen in life. It connects you to the bigger picture. Some people fight it and don't get it at all."

"I don't know if I get it but it was very unusual."

"There's more if you want to learn," Franklin said. "But not today. The rest of today is for you and Michelle. She has a lot to tell you."

"I bet she does."

"She asked me to tell you one thing that she can't quite bring herself to tell you."

"I'm not sure I want to hear this."

"I'm sure you don't. But you'll have to hear it anyway."

"Go ahead."

"She's dying," Franklin said.

Suddenly everything about the room changed. Everything about the man in front of me was different. He was a hateful, lying monster. "That's not true. I understand that she's not completely well, that something is wrong, but she can't be dying."

"We're all dying. It's just a matter of time."

"Don't give me that bullshit. Tell me about Michelle. Why did you say that?"

"Something happened to her immune system. A weakness that she was born with that allows continued damage to her nervous system. Sustained damage that is controllable to an extent but not reversible. It is only a matter of time."

I felt the world collapsing around me. "What is it called?" I asked. "The condition."

He looked a little puzzled as if he was making this all up

and he hadn't thought about a name for it. He looked out the window and then back at me and said the oddest thing. "You don't have a name for it."

"What do you mean by *I* don't have a name for it?"

"She'll have to tell you the rest. I did my part. And I'm sorry that I had to tell you. Michelle is a rare and amazing girl. That's why she's here. That's why we were willing to make an exception so she could be here with you."

I didn't know what he meant by that and I wondered who he meant by *we*. And what was this *exception* he was talking about? I saw stars as I stood up quickly and almost thought I might faint, but as I wobbled, my head cleared. I could not look at Franklin anymore. I left the room and went upstairs.

Mary was sitting with Michelle; they were talking but stopped as soon as I arrived. Mary smiled at me and got up to leave, closing the door behind her.

I sat down in the chair by Michelle and looked at her. "Tell me he's lying," I said.

"He's not. I'm sorry I couldn't tell you myself. And now I'm thinking maybe I made a mistake. I think that maybe I shouldn't have done this. I'm hurting you and I don't know why I didn't realize what would happen."

"I'm not sure I know what that all means," I said. I felt confused but there was more, much more. I put my hands on her face and I kissed her. "All I know is that I love you. There must be some way I can help."

"You can. You need to keep an open mind."

"How will that help?"

She straightened herself up. "Tell me about the meditation exercise, first."

"Why? Who cares about that?"

"Shh. Tell me if it worked."

This seemed like a silly conversation, given what we needed to talk about. "Yes," I said, "in a way, at least. I could imagine what he was saying. I could follow the instructions and it was as if I *went* somewhere."

"Your awareness went somewhere."

"Sure. Whatever."

"Then you have to let me *take* you someplace else."

"But tell me first about the illness. Tell me about why you can't be cured."

"No. Trust me."

She got up slowly and led me downstairs and back out into the forest. I followed her and it seemed that she was looking for something. I didn't know what. Finally, she stopped at a very tall pine tree with a soft mat of pine needles beneath it. "Here," she said, as she sat down and straightened her back. I followed her. "Remember how Franklin asked you to envision things. And you said you could, right?"

"Yes. I could imagine what he was saying."

"Most people can't do that easily. But you're used to using your mind to create pictures. You're a writer."

"That's my curse," I said, but I knew what she meant.

"Now, I want you to consider the possibility that not all images that come up in your mind are from your memory or from your imagination. In other words, it's possible that it's not you who is putting them there."

"Maybe."

"Think of it like reading a book. The words put the images there. Only now, I'm going to try to put the images there."

"You're going to describe something and you want me to picture it in my head?"

"No. I'm not going to speak."

"Why are we doing this?"

"You'll see. Are you ready?"

"Sure."

"Then close your eyes. And, like before, breathe. In a minute, you'll begin to see an image and then a flow of images. You need to stay relaxed and not allow your mind to question or doubt any of it."

I did as she said. For several minutes, I had a hard time calming myself. All I could think about was losing Michelle. Of her dying. It was tearing me up inside. I wanted to scream out loud. I could picture that. I could see her in a bed and I was near her, watching her breathing stop. But those were the wrong images. I knew they were being generated by my own fears. As I exhaled, I allowed those images to flow out of me and then I saw the clear, bright light again.

And then something else.

I was in another place. A city. A rather bright city with unusual buildings of many shapes and sizes. Some were famil-iar—big city glass towers—but others were of rounded shapes and made of some kind of translucent stone. And there were people, streets full of people, many of them young, and many of different shades of skin. The clothing was colorful and there was such a variety of styles that it seemed like maybe these were people from many different nations. It seemed like a cheerful, comfortable place. Something about the street scene seemed vaguely familiar.

And then I found myself walking into the lobby of one of the buildings made of translucent stone. There was no door, just a beautiful arched opening. Then, without going up any stairs or in an elevator, I could tell I was many stories above the city street. Through a window, I could see birds flying by, grackles, like the ones in my front yard. And then I was standing in front of what I now began to understand was a nurses' station. I was in a hospital. There were doctors and nurses—but they were all young.

Next I was walking into a room. The light from outside seemed to flow through the translucent stone wall and made it create beautiful living patterns in muted warm tones. A pair of doctors who appeared to be about my own age walked past me and smiled as they left.

And then I saw her, sitting up in a hospital chair. She looked bruised around the eyes and frail, but she smiled as I approached her. She smiled and held out her hand.

As soon as I touched her hand, the image disappeared.

I opened my eyes and saw that Michelle had slumped forward in front of me.

I tried to wake her but she was unconscious. At first I thought I should carry her back to the house but decided I might injure her in some way. I felt a tingling of fear in the back of my head and a sense of powerlessness. I did not understand what the images were that I had seen and how they could have seemed so real.

She opened her eyes and took a deep breath. "Sorry," she said. "I guess I lost it."

Chapter Sixteen

Michelle closed her eyes again as if she was very tired. I held her to me and listened to her shallow breathing. She was very pale and her breathing was shallow. I knew I couldn't run to get help and leave her alone. I was certain I should just wait and let her recover. Birds were singing and the sound of the water in the stream was very calming. There was wind in the tops of the trees.

I had several long minutes to try to understand what was going on. But my mind rebelled against all of it. How could she be dying? And those images in my head? Where did they come from? All I knew was that Michelle put them there somehow.

When she returned to me again, she was groggy. I smoothed her hair out of her face and I kissed her on her forehead.

"Sorry about that," she said again.

"You okay?"

"I think so."

"Should we walk back?"

"Not just yet. I need a few minutes. And you have some questions."

"They can wait," I said.

Michelle was breathing more normally now and there was color coming back into her face. "I'm not sure they can. I'm going to have to leave soon and you're going to need to know the truth."

"What do you mean, the truth?"

"Let me go at this slowly."

"Okay."

"What did you see when you closed your eyes?"

"I saw a city—the city you wanted me to see, I guess. It was unusual. Very modern but different. And the people looked different somehow. And then I was in the hospital and I saw you."

"And the doctors?"

I could still picture some of their faces. "They were quite young."

"And?"

"I don't know. It was almost like the scene was from …" But I was afraid to say it.

So she finished the sentence for me. "Almost like the scene was from your novel."

"So you were projecting this to me? Why?"

"Only it wasn't from your novel. It was real. Will be real."

"But I just imagined it—I made it up."

"No," she said. "It's real."

"You can see into the future?"

The forest seemed to suddenly go silent. No birds, no wind, no stream. But it must have been the sound of the blood pumping in my ears, blocking it all out.

"I'm from the future," Michelle said.

I looked into her eyes, but I could not focus properly on her. I waited for her to smile, to tell me it was a joke. But she didn't.

I sat silently and waited.

"I felt bad, lying to you."

"You said you were from California."

"I am."

"But the California of the future?"

"Yes."

"How?"

"I'll try to explain later. I promise."

"But you came here and I fell in love with you."

"I didn't think that would happen."

"But why did you come here?"

"Because of you."

"Why me?"

"Because you wrote the novel."

"You read my novel *before* it was written?"

"Technically, it was *after* it was written. Long after."

I felt dizzy and a little nauseous. Could any of this possibly be true? I felt like there must be some bizarre conspiracy. Maybe Michelle and her crazy aunt and uncle had involved me in some strange sort of mind game, some warped kind of experiment. "You want me to believe that you traveled through time to get here?"

"Yes."

"Who else is from the future?"

"Franklin and Mary."

"What about Mr. Clayton? What about Botzweiler? What about my parents?"

"No, none of them."

I looked around to see if anyone was watching us. A hidden audience? A camera? There had to be some explanation other than what she was telling me.

"Close your eyes again," she said.

"No." I wouldn't do it. "No more mind games."

"They aren't mind games. Sometimes it's easier to see than to explain."

"I think I'll keep my eyes open."

"I'm sorry I couldn't tell you the truth before this."

"What else are you lying about? Are you really sick? Or was that just to get my sympathy?" The dizziness returned. I was feeling very vulnerable now. Very used. But at the same time, I wanted her to tell me the sickness thing was a lie. I so desperately wanted that.

"Unfortunately, that's the truth. And it's partly why I am here."

"If you're from the future, why don't they have some futuristic cure for what's killing you?"

"Because some problems can't be solved. Some things can't be cured. You suggested that in your novel. Your troubleshooters—like Austin. He could improve things, make things better, but he couldn't 'cure' Krieg. I guess you were prophetic about that, too."

"Prophetic? I was just writing a novel. I took an idea and I explored it."

"And, whether you like it or not, you laid down a kind of blueprint for the way the world could be."

"I refuse to believe that," I said. This was way too insane.

Michelle held my hand. I almost pulled back but I didn't. "This is a hell of a lot for you to swallow all at once. And it's going to get weirder before it's over."

"But I'm supposed to keep an open mind, right?"

She leaned forward and I think she was going to kiss me but I pulled back.

"Yes. Can you do that?"

"I don't know."

"Okay, you want to know why I'm here. I'll tell you. I read your novel when I was thirteen. I wanted so much to meet the person who wrote it. I asked about other books by you but there were none. A lot of people didn't think your book was all that great but almost everyone knew how significant it was in setting off a chain of events. The youth rights movement. The age discrimination legislation. You were the catalyst."

"Botzweiler and the book and all the media hype and all that?"

"It's only the beginning. Maybe things might have gone the way they did without your book. Some people debate that. Your book was at the center of what became a huge controversy. But the voting age was lowered once, and then a second time, and then it was a tidal wave that couldn't be stopped. In the end, it was the adults, though, who mostly believed it was the right thing to do."

"Turn the decision-making over to young people?"

"Yes. It was a long transition. And it's not at all exactly as in your novel. But the concept is there. Start working young after serious preparation. Work through five to eight of your best years of physical ability and intellectual insight and then choose your own future—stay on as an advisor or simply enjoy the rest of your life and let younger people take on the responsibilities."

"The doctors?"

"Yes. Trained young, in charge by the time they're sixteen."

"But they haven't been able to help you?"

"They have been able to help. There just wasn't any real solution."

"How did they help?"

"The whole time travel thing came about from young people thinking outside the box or, as you say, living outside the lines. It requires a huge amount of energy, though, so it is mostly banned. And some are still a little concerned about things going wrong—altering the time line and that sort of thing."

"Then why did they let you come here? Seems like a pretty big gamble."

"Well, it was Franklin and Mary, when they were in their teens, who mastered the technique. It was a combination of mental abilities and technology. They were the first to use it—before they even told anyone about it. And it seems not to have altered anything. But they've kept themselves and the use of their process quite limited. It's used only in the rarest cases, after considerable scrutiny."

"But why did you get to use it?"

"Because some of those troubleshooters—like Austin, young people from various disciplines—got together to see what could be done to help me since all else had failed. My nervous system was continuing to degenerate. One believed that if I was living outside my own time, I might be able to live longer. During the time when I was not in my own present I would not continue to get worse."

"So that's why you came here?"

"Yes. But I can only stay for a limited time. And I've already overstayed what was considered to be safe."

"But why here? Why now?"

"Like I said—because of you. I told them I wanted to go back and be with you."

"Risking some alteration in the past and maybe altering the future?"

She smiled and her face softened. "That was the funny part about all this."

"Funny? How could any of this be funny?"

"It didn't take much digging on anybody's part to discover that I was already here."

My head was swirling again. "Explain."

"As soon as the troubleshooting team began to look into the archives—they began to discover that there was a girl. You had a girlfriend when you were sixteen. She had been in that all-important creative writing class. She'd read your early drafts of the novel."

"And that was you."

"It was me."

Chapter Seventeen

That night when I was in bed with Michelle, she pulled me towards her and started kissing me passionately. "Make love to me," she said.

"Are you sure it's okay?" I responded. I wanted to badly but was worried about her condition. In truth, I felt embarrassed when I had to say that it would be my first time.

"Mine too," she said. "I'm considered to be quite odd where I come from. And yes, it's most definitely okay."

I was suddenly nervous and shy but once we began to kiss again, there was nothing to hold us back.

We stayed for one more day and I allowed Franklin and,

later, Mary to guide me with several meditation exercises. Part of me still wondered if everything happening here at the cabin was a crazy mind-control exercise dreamed up by a couple of demented psychologists. Another part of me, however, was beginning to accept that this was real. But I was having a very hard time getting my head around what would happen in the days ahead. The worst of it was that, one way or the other, I was losing Michelle. She would go away and I would never see her again.

Mary tried to explain something of the nature of time travel—its possibilities, dangers, and limitations. She tried to explain some of the technical side but it was way over my head. "Let me put it another way," she said, after failing to help me grasp how some of the *old* laws of physics could *bend*. "If we didn't live our lives as if they were linear, most of us would go crazy. So we see time as a single line moving from the past into the future. But even some of the ancient philosophers saw time as an illusion. They talked about the past, the present, and the future existing all at once. If you only had the means, you could drop from one into the other. We just never had the means until we started looking for the threads between mind, memory, and the kind of time anomalies that exist in deep space. When we realized we could create those same physical conditions on earth, it opened up some doors. We just weren't sure what to do if we walked through those doors. So we proceeded *very* cautiously."

"Then you can move into the future if you wanted to, as well as the past?"

Franklin walked into the room then with a pot of tea. He poured some into cups and I sipped cautiously. "We said no. We wouldn't attempt to go into the future. Too risky. The past is bad enough."

"So you've only traveled into the past?"

"Yes," Franklin answered. "And, even then, very cautiously, with great diligence. We only go into the past if we have evidence … well, that we were already there."

"Yes," Mary added. "Michelle probably told you. We found out that she was already part of the storyline."

"Then you can tell me what happens next?"

"We'd prefer not to," Franklin said firmly. "We still believe in free will. You have to choose your path. We could not choose it for you."

"But, in a way, if I understand what you are saying, it is already chosen."

"Yes, it is," Mary said. "But chosen by you."

"Would Michelle live longer if she stayed here outside of her time line?"

"No," Franklin said. "She wouldn't. Her stay here has extended her life but only as far as it was possible. The remaining care she needs now is back in her home."

"And how long will she survive there?"

"Four months possibly. Six at the most. The good news is that, with the available treatment, her quality of life will be quite good right up to near the end." He seemed far too clinical in the way he was saying this.

"How can you be so matter-of-fact about it?" I asked.

Mary cleared her throat. "Nigel, we love her. She is like our own child. The only way we've been able to help her is by doing this. We weren't even sure we should be here until we saw the footage of your speech. We were there in the audience."

"What speech?"

"Oops," Mary said.

"Oops is right," Franklin added.

When I arrived home, my parents were quite upset. "We had people walking around with picket signs in front of the house last night," my mom said. "I don't understand it."

"I want that damn publisher to pull the book off the shelves," my dad said, looking totally flustered.

"Has he called?"

"Several times. The man is a lunatic. And he's really riled

that you are not returning his calls. I don't like him at all. We're going to have the phone number changed. Then all the wackos won't be able to get through. And who is this Gary guy who keeps showing up here?"

"Gary? Oh, him. He's nobody." Just what I needed—a pain in the butt like Mr. Save the World. If I wasn't careful, I'd end up getting the crap beaten out of me like he did.

I looked at my poor confused parents. "I'm really sorry about this."

"Your teacher, Mr. Clayton, called. We unloaded on him. He said he had no idea this would happen. He said he'd talk to Botzweiler."

"Botzweiler won't listen. He probably loves the fact that the book is both popular and pissing people off."

Right then, I felt bad for my parents but all I could really focus on was the fact that the time I had left with Michelle was limited. Very limited. Franklin wouldn't say exactly but it was only a matter of days and they'd be gone. "Mom, Dad, I'm going to stay at Michelle's for a few days—so no one can find me. Don't tell anyone I'm there, please. And you guys should maybe go away for a bit. Stay at a hotel or something."

"But we love you and we're worried about you," my mom said. She was about to cry. "You're too young for all this. We don't want you to get hurt. You're not ready for any of this."

I understood what she was saying but, right then, at that moment, I did not feel young at all. My mind was completely clear and I realized I could keep all the turmoil around me, all that was out there in the world and all the doubts and fears within me—I could hold it at a distance, away from me. And at the center of my being, I knew there was only one thing to do. Go and be with Michelle. For as long as I could.

"I'm going to be okay," I said. "And I love you both."

My mother started crying then and I hugged her. I hugged my father, too, and he was rather awkward hugging me back. I had the haunting feeling that I might not ever see them again.

My father offered to drive me but I said I wanted to walk.

I didn't get very far before I was ambushed by Gary.

"Nigel," he said. "You're the torch, man. You lit the flame."

"I told you, it's just a novel. I don't really understand what everyone is getting heated up about." I kept walking but he was there in my face at every step. The guy must have been watching the house, waiting for me to return. Stalking me.

"We need you for the movement," he said. "We've all read your book. It is so cool. And better yet, everyone is reading it."

"But how come some people hate it?"

"It scares the shit out of them. You're talking about something that will change everything."

"Maybe everything doesn't need changing," I said. But then I thought about what Michelle had shown me, the things she'd told me about her world. A world that already existed, somehow, even though it was in the future.

"It does. And it needs to change before it's too late."

I saw some people watching us now, some of the neighbors in front of a house. One guy pointed at us. At me. And then he yelled something. I didn't understand it but it wasn't nice.

"See what I mean. You scare them. And they deserve to be scared."

I knew I wasn't going to blow this guy off easily, but he was sure annoying me. And I didn't want him to know where I was headed, so I turned down a side street, heading away from Frank and Mary's place. "Who deserves to be scared?" I asked.

"All those people who vote for the same old politicians who say the same old crap. The ones who lead us into war. The ones who hold to the status quo. The ones who keep the rich people rich and the truly poor people poor. And there's a hell of a lot of them out there."

"And what is it *you* want?" I asked him. My take on Gary was that he just wanted to cause trouble. How exactly I ended up on his side of this battle was beyond me.

"I'm not alone on this. The first thing we want to do is lower the voting age. Then we mobilize young voters to get some new blood into all levels of government. And we start giving back the rights that have been denied young people for the last century."

"Did you ever think that some of us just maybe like being young and not having so many responsibilities?"

Gary grabbed my wrist and then just stopped. He was really pissing me off now.

He looked me in the eye. "Yeah, I understand that. I just don't think we can afford that for much longer."

I didn't want anything to do with his cause. I wanted to be with Michelle, but there were things connecting in my brain. Now that I knew a certain future existed, I realized there were specific things I was *supposed* to do. And what if I failed to do them?

"This is way too much responsibility for me."

Gary pulled out one of his famous green pamphlets. "Take this. It's tomorrow. If you would just show up and talk about your book ... well, it could mean a hell of a lot to a lot of good people." And he turned and walked away.

I opened the pamphlet and read about a rally taking place in front of City Hall tomorrow. An age discrimination demonstration. I read the hype and didn't much like the tone of it. I was about to toss it when it sunk in. A speech. I was being asked to give a speech.

When I arrived at Michelle's, I told her about my encounter with Gary. She immediately understood the implications.

"What if I decide not to give the speech?" I asked.

"I don't really know what happens then. There's so much about the time line we don't understand."

"But I have to give this speech, right?"

"You have to do what you feel is the right thing to do. I can't influence you on that."

"But you already have. So you might as well tell me what happens next."

"No. It doesn't work that way. I know it's confusing. Franklin and Mary think that we need to leave very soon."

"I know. And I can't bear the thought of living without you."

She smiled a soft smile and touched my face. I was certain I was about to lose her for good. She would go back to her world and she would live for a few more months and then she would die. And me? What exactly would become of me?

So I sat alone in her living room and wrote a speech— not a great speech, but something that I could offer to who- ever showed up. I tried to show it to Michelle but she said she shouldn't read it. She explained that she would be there with her aunt and uncle but that I should go there on my own.

There were a couple of hundred people that evening gathered round the front steps of City Hall. I'd never been to a protest rally before. There were adults in the crowd but it was mostly teenagers. Quite a few university students as well. A lot of the faces in the crowd looked angry. I wasn't expecting that. TV crews were there and so were police.

I felt out of place and very alone as I wandered into the crowd. I noticed that a few of the kids were carrying around a copy of my book. A couple of them were holding it up in the air as if it were some kind of symbol. And then Gary spotted me. He rushed over and gave me a hug. He was all smiles now. "Thanks for coming, Nigel," he said. And then he ushered me towards a makeshift stage on the steps of City Hall. He introduced me to some other university students who smiled, shook my hand, and patted me on the back as if we were old friends.

After about ten minutes of small talk, Gary said it was time to begin. He went up to the microphone and raised a fist in the air. The crowd now had grown to about three hundred. Fists went up into the air and people cheered, and then the crowd went silent. He didn't say much—just thanked people for coming and began to introduce the first speaker. Oddly enough it was an old guy—a retired history professor who looked to be at least seventy. Dr. Arthur Gorman.

"In my lifetime," he said, "I've watched war ravage nations over and over again. I've watched world leaders who prey on people's fears guide their citizens into paths of destruction. I've watched health care decline in this country and I've seen people living in poverty and neglect, even as the economy raced forward. It seems that, in my generation, we've hit a snag where social equality has not moved forward, and so we stagnate. The suffragette movement, the civil rights movement, the gay rights movement—all took us in the right direction to give rights and privileges to the disenfranchised. But then something happened. We failed to extend those rights to one of the most important and largest segments of our population—our youth." He paused, looked up and around. "But that's all about to change. We're here tonight as one of hundreds of rallies going on across North America and beyond. We're here to voice our demand to lower the voting age and extend rights of adulthood to young people."

A massive cheer went up. I had one hand in my pocket, holding onto my speech as I looked out at the crowd. I scanned the faces and saw no one I knew, at first. And then

I spotted Franklin with Mary beside him. And then I saw Michelle. But she was too far off for me to make eye contact with her. Suddenly, I felt very, very nervous. I wanted to run away. But it was too late.

And then Gorman continued. "And now I'd like to introduce an extraordinary young man who is the author of a daring new novel that gives us a vision of a world that could be some day—not a perfect world, but an improved one. I welcome Nigel Lukes."

Gorman walked over to me, put an arm around my shoulder in a fatherly way, and led me to the microphone. The crowd cheered wildly and some people held my book up into the air. I felt panic rising inside me as I took my folded handwritten speech out of my pocket. What I had to offer was not that much. I was not a speechmaker. I was a kid who had written a book. I was filled with self doubts as I looked up and away. The crowd grew quiet. I looked towards the back until I could spot Michelle again. I knew I had to make this speech. Something about this moment made her world possible. And so it helped make her possible.

I took a deep breath and found myself focusing on that breath, as Franklin had taught me in his meditation coaching. Had he been preparing me for just this moment? I closed my eyes and took a second breath. I thought I saw a bright light instead of a crowd of faces and the light enveloped me and made me calm. And then I opened my eyes to the now silent crowd and began.

"I'm not exactly sure how I ended up here tonight. I didn't write a book to make anybody want to lower the voting age or change the world. In truth, I wrote it as a kind of escape from reality. I created a fantasy world and I lived there while I was writing it. It was more exciting than school or TV or playing video games." A few people laughed and then there was silence again. I looked at the TV cameras—three of them at least, all aimed at me.

"But I wrote the book because it was one of the first real chances I had to show what I could do, to prove what I was capable of. All my life I felt that I had been held back. I don't really mean in a personal way. It wasn't my parents or my teachers or even the law. It was just the way things were. As kids, we're protected and cared for and this goes on from the time we're little to the time we are teenagers, and when we are ready to try something big—to grow beyond child-hood—something holds us back. Wait until you are older, those voices say. You're too young.

"So I had this teacher who gave me this little window of opportunity to do something big. To write a story, a novel. And I leaped through that window, knowing that if I fell, it wouldn't hurt all that much. I'd fail the course or fail to write a novel. I'd give up and feel like a loser. But I was given an opportunity. And when I leaped out that window, I didn't fall. I flew. I wrote a novel about the future and it seemed so real, it was like I was living it.

"It's a work of the imagination. It's not the way things will be. It's not a prediction or a game plan. But now that it's published as a book, and people are reacting, I can see that I tapped into something that many people were thinking about. When we are young, our skills and abilities are wasted. We are deprived of the right to help shape the future. And that's wrong." That was the end of my speech but it was like the crowd was waiting for something more. So I added this: "And that should change."

As soon as I turned from the microphone, people began to cheer. Before I could go a few steps, Dr. Gorman took my arm and raised it into the air as if I'd just won some kind of prizefight. I looked out at the crowd and saw the sea of fists raised into the air. I don't know what made me do it, but I made a fist as well. I got carried away in the moment.

Gary wanted me to stay around up front but I had to leave. As I made my way through the crowd, a few kids held their copies of my book out to me to sign but I waved them away. I needed to get to Michelle. I was afraid that I would never see her again. The speech had been given. It would appear on the news and be on-line. That was enough. Maybe now would be the time for them to make their exit. And there was more to it than that as well. Maybe I really did believe what I'd said in the speech. I didn't know if it was possible. But I had one more window I was ready to leap out of.

Chapter Eighteen

So this is what it was like to have fans, I thought, as I continued to wave book-wielding well-wishers away. I saw one of the TV cameras still tracking me as I threaded my way towards the rear of the crowd. A couple of angry protesters were taunting the police and I wondered how long the cops would tolerate that. I began to run to get away from them. I ran to where I'd seen Michelle, Franklin, and Mary. But they were gone.

I felt the panic rising in me. I ran across the street, only to discover that I had put myself right in the middle of a group of counter-demonstrators. They held placards denouncing the rights movement. They looked angry and they knew exactly who I was and had heard what I had to say. I paused for a minute, my pathway blocked. I saw loathing in their distorted faces; I had never had to stare at anyone in my life who hated me like this. Why were they here? I wondered. Why did my novel frighten them so? I felt like a cornered animal.

And then a woman of about thirty stepped forward with my book held up in her hand. I didn't understand at first. I looked around behind me, searching for my escape route. I noticed one of the cameramen stumble, then recover as he moved forward to stand within a few feet of me. His camera was dead on her. And then she lit a rolled piece of newspaper and held it up to the book until it caught fire. "This is what I think of your book," the woman said, her face contorted by her hatred of me.

And, as all eyes were on the burning book, my book, I turned and ran down the street.

I ran a few blocks and then jumped on the first bus that would take me closer to Michelle's house. I was winded and collapsed into a seat near the front. There were only a handful of people on the bus and no one seemed to know or care who I was. I got off three blocks from Michelle's and, having gotten my wind back, ran to her doorstep. I walked in without knocking.

There was no one there. Damn.

I climbed the stairs and opened the door to Michelle's bedroom.

She was lying down and Mary was holding her wrist, taking her pulse.

"I'm glad you're here, Nigel," Franklin said. "Damn good speech. Now it's time for us to say goodbye."

"No," I said. "Not yet."

Mary nodded at Michelle. She didn't have to say it. Michelle looked weak. I understood that if she stayed here, she wouldn't live much longer.

Michelle looked tired but her eyes were open. "I was so proud of you," she said.

"I always hated having to speak in front of the class at school. That was like my worst nightmare."

"You did what you had to do. And now we have to go back."

I can't precisely tell you what I was feeling right then. Fear was the biggest part of it. Fear of losing Michelle. But that fear of loss came from the fact that I loved her so much. There would never be any girl like her in my life.

"I can't go back to being just a kid anymore after tonight, can I?" I asked Franklin.

"I wouldn't know," he said.

"I'll be hounded by those who think I'm their guru and those who think I'm out to destroy everything they know and love."

"You'll be okay," Michelle said. "You're strong."

"I don't think I want to be strong. I don't know what I want anymore."

"Don't worry. Things will begin to make a bit more sense soon. I promise."

"We need to leave tonight," Mary said. "I'm sorry."

I settled into the bed alongside of Michelle and I put my arms around her. Franklin and Mary took the hint. "We'll be downstairs," Franklin told Michelle. "Let us know when you're ready. We'll have everything prepared." And they left us alone.

"I'm thinking about a love story," I said, picking up on what Michelle said. "I'm thinking about two people who really love each other and find themselves in an impossible situation where they can't be together."

She smiled and folded herself in to me. "It's been done before. *Romeo and Juliet* and about a thousand other stories."

I held her close to me. "Like Clayton said, there's just no such thing as a new plot. It's all been done before. But not like this. I've got several possible endings. The happy one doesn't seem to work. All the rest are sad—tragic, even— but one reads better than the rest."

"Which one is that?" I could feel her breath against my neck and I could feel warm, wet tears on me.

"The one that breaks all the rules. He goes with her to wherever she has to go."

"You can't do that. It's not permitted."

"Who makes up the rules?"

She didn't answer.

"Probably a bunch of know-nothing teenagers," I said. "But is it possible?"

She sat upright and looked at me. "I thought about it. I even discussed it with Franklin and Mary."

"And?"

"They wouldn't give me a straight answer."

"Why?"

"I'm not sure. But then I thought that even if it were possible, you could never, ever return to this, your own time line."

"I think I knew that. I couldn't go into the future, see what the future would be like, and then return here, knowing what I know."

"Right. And that would mean you'd be marooned in the future, my present."

"Doesn't sound so bad to me," I said.

"But you'd never see your parents again. And they wouldn't know what happened to you."

"That's the worst of it. It would be cruel. They've been good to me. It's going to tear them up. And I'll miss them.

I mean, I've thought about moving out someday, being on my own. But this is different. I'd be abandoning them … well, forever." Now I felt like I was about to cry. "But I could do it. I love you, remember?"

"But you're forgetting something."

"No. I'm not. If what you say is true, I'd have you for … what? Four months, half a year?"

"Yes. That part is all true. There is no miracle cure and no more travel through time for me. *My* future has been thoroughly established. The doctors have slowed the progress of the condition but they cannot stop it. I refused to accept it at first. But now I can see the truth."

"Then you've already been able to actually see into your future and know exactly what will happen?"

"No. Not like that. Remember, we never, ever use the travel technique to move forward into our own future. Everyone agrees the results could be disastrous—or at least very uncertain and risky."

"But your past is already fixed. Everything that happened today, that happened so far, was *supposed* to happen?"

"We don't really look at it that way. But what happened today fits with what we could research. The rally and the fact we were there. Your speech."

"You read my speech before I wrote it?"

"Technically, it was long after you wrote it."

"Right."

"Michelle?" It was Franklin calling from downstairs.

"I want to go with you. I don't care if I can't come back. I love you."

"And I love you, Nigel. But it would be so unfair to you. It would be so selfish on my part."

"Please let me do this. I can't stay here. I can't lose you. Help me convince Franklin and Mary."

And then a strange sequence of events occurred. Franklin and Mary put up no protest whatsoever.

"But you have to write your parents a letter—a handwritten letter. Not an e-mail. And you have to mail it." Mary rummaged around in a desk and found paper, a pen, a business envelope, and a stamp. "Sit. Write," she said.

It was harder than I thought. Saying goodbye to them. Explaining that I was okay but that they might not see me again. I told them I loved them and always would and apologized for doing this, but that I really would be okay. I made it sound like it had something to do with the popularity of the book and the rights movement. They would still know that something was very, very odd. But it was the best I could do.

"Now mail it," Franklin said. I walked out of the house

and to the corner to a mailbox and dropped the letter in. As I turned to go back, I became certain that I would open the door to an empty house. It was their way of getting me out of there so they could leave.

I held my breath as I opened the door.

I was wrong. They were all sitting on the floor, legs crossed, backs straight, in a meditation pose. In the center of the floor was a silver box, something that looked like a laptop computer. And Mary had in front of her a medical kit with four small syringes like the kind I'd seen diabetics use. "We've found that the only way to do this properly without serious confusion and mental trauma is to be unconscious. I hope you aren't afraid of needles."

That part did throw me off. Was it a trick after all? I'd be rendered unconscious and when I woke they'd all be gone? Or was it more bizarre than that? Some sort of suicide ritual. Maybe we'd all be found dead. Maybe no one was from the future. Maybe it was all some crazy hyped-up game.

Michelle looked very worried. "You can still change your mind. Once we are injected, there will be no turning back."

I searched her face for the truth.

And found it. I knew I had to trust her or there was nothing in this world I could ever trust again.

"I want to be with you," I said.

I watched Mary give the first needle to Michelle and saw her close her eyes and begin to fall asleep. Then she injected me and I felt the sharp needle pierce my skin. But there was no panic. The fear was all gone. Franklin simply tapped once on the laptop device and held his arm out. Mary injected him and then herself.

And then everything went black.

Chapter Nineteen

Within two years, Jonathan Krieg had been released. No one ever used words like "cured," but he was deemed fit by a team of five young psychiatrists, who determined that he was capable of returning to society and that he would be "adopted" by a team of young pain researchers to provide advice and possibly write about his past work and his experience.

As he had been Austin's very first case, Austin felt a certain pride in having dealt with a very difficult situation. He had grown to like and even admire Krieg. And he had learned something about how even good people sometimes commit terrible acts and how everyone involved can ultimately move onward rather than wallowing in self-pity and punishment.

Austin's own youthful insecurities had been replaced by a calm dignity, confidence, and knowledge that allowed him to move freely into other fields to use his troubleshooting skills. His long talks with Krieg had led him to move out of counseling and into medicine. Krieg, despite the fact he was a murderer, had become a kind of mentor to Austin, who then teamed up with a group of fifteen-year-olds, fresh out of med school, who pooled interests in various traditional and nontraditional medical fields to look for ways to expand the potential of the human brain. Austin became somewhat of an expert on being able to create bridges between very disparate fields of research and provide solutions to problems—especially medical problems—from some of the most unlikely sources.

By the time he was eighteen, he found himself looking around for even greater challenges and consulting with some officials rather high up in government circles, who wanted to pick his brain about everything from the all-important prep years, where children are trained to move into their active phase, as well as issues involving fuelless transportation, international food, and population issues. It was from those government contacts that he was thrust into the world of international diplomacy.

Tamara and Austin were talking about having their first child. Tamara was already twenty-one and finishing her last year of full employment. She loved children and was a wonderful teacher, and like most men and women about to move on to the next phase, she wondered if it was the right thing to do. Turn the work over to the next generation, that is. Almost everyone about to move forward had some doubts. Would the next younger generation do things differently? Would they want to do things their own way and ignore all the hard work that had come before them? Would they turn their back on traditional ways of doing things? On knowledge? On history? These were natural worries.

But Austin had been part of a national council that had reassured the public that continuity was not as big an issue as innovation. The pattern had been established from early on that each successive generation would naturally find ways to keep what worked of the old ways, to build upon them with innovation, and to reject what was irrelevant or rooted in the past but not applicable to the future.

Tamara and Austin looked forward to a long life—raising two children, living by the sea, exploring creative projects like writing, painting, and music. But their current livelihood still filled their days with plentiful challenges.

There were certain large-scale problems, so large in scope that even the best troubleshooters of the enlightened nations could not begin to solve them without cooperation with the old republics. Climate issues left over from the early twenty-first century were still of grave concern and there were still disastrous food short-ages for the poorer nations. The older republics, the ones still run by a kind of patriarchal system of democracy that preferred to elect old men (and a few older women), still saw the younger nations as a threat, and many refused to follow the lead of the newer technologies and social engineering theories.

The world was still divided into many camps. Fundamentalist religions still dominated many nations. Old-style free enterprise capitalism was entrenched in much of the old U.S. and nations in Asia. Despite their significant differences, they all shared a fear and mistrust of the newer forward-looking nations, and the pace at which things changed in the new nations scared them even more.

It was into that arena that Austin was thrust with his consider-able interfacing expertise. There had been considerable research advanced about the means to actually reverse the global climate shifts that had made for worsening droughts in Australia and sub-Saharan Africa and intensified storm activity in the northeast Atlantic and Pacific northwest of North America. There was talk of massive volunteer tree-replanting initiatives in the far north and in South America, and a final and absolute worldwide ban on the use of any fuels that emitted CO_2.

MidAmerica was the most powerful and vociferous opponent of such activity despite the fact that drought there had changed the nature of farming into something that was more truly agricultural manufacturing—just barely surviving through the use of deep-drill irrigation and chemical fertilizers.

Austin was away from home in Nebraska, meeting with American politicians to discuss some solutions to these big issues, when a truly horrendous mega-storm struck the coastal town that was his home. Tamara had been coming home to their apartment when the sea swept up over the breakwater and flooded the shorelines. She was swept out to sea and not seen again.

All that they had planned for in their upcoming years would never happen. Austin was not at all prepared for this. He returned home to face up to the greatest challenge of his life. He realized that he could not begin to "fix" anything about his life. He asked for an early dismissal from his work and a chance to drop out of his profession. The request was granted and so began Austin's lonely, dark vigil, as he brooded over all the problems of the world that were now seemingly unfixable.

He suffered from severe depression, and found himself contacting, of all people, Jonathan Krieg.

Krieg and Austin became close friends, and it was Krieg who talked Austin out of ending his life. "Give it another month," he said. "All it takes is time."

It didn't seem like time would heal those wounds. And as Austin watched the news—more food rioting, more natural catastrophes—he began to lose faith that the new order of youth was capable of dealing with problems of this magnitude.

And then one day Krieg showed up with a man of about sixty who introduced himself as a Warren Bourgese, special advisor to the president of MidAmerica.

"We've reached a critical point in the Senate," Warren said, "where enough senators have become sympathetic to anti-age discrimination that I think we could make the change. I think we must make the change. We need to learn from what you have to offer."

"But you need to hear from the young ones. Not me. I'm twenty-two and I'm no longer active in anything professionally."

"Perhaps that's why we need to hear from you first. Because you are not so young. But you'll still be addressing much older people. In order for there to be a peaceful transition, the old will have to hand things over to the young."

"As it should be," Austin said.

"We met before," Warren said. "You don't remember me, though. Maybe that's good. We were quite opposed to those grandiose schemes you proposed to us. Now we know better."

"But then you'll have to be open to what they have to offer." It was understood who they were.

"Some of us know that. Some of us are starting to see the larger picture. China, for example, needs our grains. The rice shortage is beyond critical. And if we are able to orchestrate the change, then I think it will move them in a similar direction."

And so Austin was drawn out of his self-imposed retirement for the next two years and found himself living in the middle of the *continent in a society that went through the most gentle revolution known on the face of the earth. Before long, the three other old North American republics moved in that direction as well.*

When he bowed out of public service, Austin was truly ready for what was ahead—not exactly a life of leisure and happiness, but a time of reflection and solace, and a chance to sit back and let the next generation surprise the older ones again and again with the promise of new ideas, new growth in all fields, an ongoing revolution of the mind and of the spirit.

Chapter Twenty

When I opened my eyes, I saw the sky. It was a clear blue with wispy clouds. I was lying on my back on the ground. Green grass was beneath me, and as I turned my head I saw flowers. I was in a garden. Or at least I thought I was in a garden. Or possibly dead.

I did not move at first. And then when I tried to move, I felt pain in my joints. I moved my neck first and then raised my arms. My muscles felt stiff and uncooperative. A bit more pain but nothing serious. The discomfort most certainly meant that I was alive.

Around me were trees with shimmering green leaves, flowering bushes, and sunlight everywhere. But not a sign of anything that indicated there were other people around. I sat up finally and blinked into the bright sun.

And then she appeared. Michelle, walking towards me across the grass. She didn't say a word but held out her hands to help me up. She looked younger than I remembered and healthier.

"So, I'm here?" I asked.

"Yes. Do you like it?"

"What's not to like?" I touched her face and kissed her on the mouth. It felt like the two of us were alone in the Garden of Eden.

"You okay?" she asked when I drew back and rubbed my neck.

"A little sore—all over."

"Everyone reacts differently to the travel. For me, that time, I felt energized. I awoke feeling better than I had for a long time."

"Not me. But I'll be okay. Where am I?"

"In the garden behind my house. I was only gone a few minutes. I've been keeping an eye on you, don't worry. This is where we arrived back. I've been up for a while. But you were still out and it's better to let someone wake on their own."

My eyes were starting to focus now and I could hear my own blood pounding in my ears. I couldn't believe I was really in the future, in Michelle's world. The air I breathed into my lungs seemed invigorating and wonderful. I forgot about my minor aches and pains and looked wide-eyed at the beauty of the trees and flowers around me. "This is incredible," I said out loud with a smile.

"This is your new home."

"When do I get to see the rest of your world?"

"Not yet. Franklin is discussing your issue with the Council."

"So I'm under house arrest?"

"Something like that."

"And you are my jailer?"

"Yes."

Michelle lived alone in what I would call a small but very modern cottage made of that translucent stone I had seen in the vision she had projected to me. She revealed to me what she had been trained to do—a kind of counselor for children with terminal illnesses. "Ever since my own diagnosis," she said, "which was when I was twelve, I knew I would live a shorter life than most. I decided I would accept that and make the absolute most of it. Franklin and Mary helped train me. After that, it was the children who trained me. And I counseled them. "

"What I can't seem to understand," I said, "is that if

you've made so many advances, why are there still children dying? Why do you have to die?"

She sighed. "That's one of the hardest things to understand for all of us. But it comes down to the fact that there is no perfect world. There will always be some pain, some suffering. And death. There will always be death. But many people live to be over a hundred now. It's quite common. Some live out their old age in comfort, some in misery. Some die when they choose."

That struck a dark chord in me. "Assisted suicide? Euthanasia?"

"Old terms that no longer exist. No matter what age, if someone says they would like to end their life, they go to a retreat with their own personal guide. I was one of those guides for a while. Mary had been one when she was younger. The retreat is for anyone of any age, old or young. Most decide they want to live afterwards. Very few, mostly those older ones in pain that can't be alleviated, choose to die, and they do so gracefully and with dignity."

"I still don't like the sound of it. No matter how civilized you make it appear."

"You grew up in a different time and place."

"Will there be many things like this that will be hard for me to understand?"

"There will be some."

"When do I find out if I can go out into the world?"

"You're tired of being locked up with me already?"

"Never," I said.

It was a week before Franklin came for a visit to say that, after considerable debate, it was determined I could travel about freely in the city and countryside. Governing councilors and temporal science experts had put forward dozens of good reasons why I should live the rest of my days in isolation, but they were so appalled by notions of restraint and confinement that they had to set me free.

"No one was afraid I might somehow propagate old ideas, old ways?"

"We know about all the old ways, remember?" Franklin said. "We have history."

Franklin had that funny look on his face, the one he had when I had first met him and I thought he was a little crazy.

He turned to Michelle. "Do you have any beer?"

Michelle rolled her eyes slightly and left the room.

"But how important, really, was my book? Do people out there really know about me?"

Franklin smiled an impish grin. "We think of you as a god," he said.

I guess I must have looked stunned.

"Just kidding," he said. "Some people would know about you. Some never would have heard about you or your book. Michelle was the exception. She knew everything about you."

"Kind of stalking me through time?" I said, just as she came back into the room with a couple of glasses of beer.

"How does that make you feel?" she asked.

"Flattered," I said.

"Once it was determined that we could extend her life if she made one foray back to somewhere, she chose to be in your time and place. She wanted to be with you."

"The rest," Michelle added, "as they say, is history."

"I'm the luckiest person in the world," I said. "But I can't believe my book is still in print." And then I thought more about it. "I can't believe there still are books around."

"Books are artifacts. People still buy actual books, sometimes just to hold one in their hands as they read. They say they like the tactile pleasure of it."

"But the book," I said. "My book. It's not that good. It has a few ideas in it. I still don't understand what all the fuss was about."

"It's not that bad," Michelle said in defense of it. "It made me want to meet the person who wrote it. It made me fall in love with you, I think, even before I met you."

I changed my opinion. "Damn. Then I think it is a masterpiece."

Franklin sipped his beer. "Believe me, the literary scholars have a field day with your book. A few defend it as a classic. Most suggest it's little more than a political comic book."

"Ouch," I said.

"Down through history, books that were not particularly well written have proven to have a powerful impact," Franklin said. "*Pilgrim's Progress, Das Kapital, Mein Kampf,* the works of Sigmund Freud. You're in both good and bad company. Like many of those books, though, yours appeared at a unique time and captured the interest of the public who were debating those issues of youth rights. And then, to seal your place in history ... " he stopped to slurp down some more beer, "... you disappeared."

The reality of that swept back over me like a thunderstorm. "I did, didn't I? My parents? Do you know anything about what happened to them?"

"Yes," Michelle said. "They were harassed by the media for weeks. They had to move. But then they started fresh. They adopted an orphaned girl from China."

"They moved on?"

"Yes. They loved you. They missed you. But ultimately they had to assume you were dead. And then they got on with their lives."

"As everybody has to do," Franklin added. "It's the only

way." I think I knew then that he was talking about me. About what lay ahead for me.

"Are you regretting that you came here?" Michelle asked. She could read my every look.

"No," I said. "I'm glad I'm here. I just feel badly about what I did to my parents."

"That was a long time ago," Franklin suggested.

"Long ago, but not very far away in my memory," I said. "Funny the things you'll do for love."

Michelle looked sad now. I knew, too, what she was thinking.

"It was my decision," I said. "Six months with you or a lifetime without you. Wasn't very hard to choose at all."

"I think I'll be going," Franklin said. "Thanks for the beer."

There were long walks in the countryside and days wandering in the city. At every turn, there was a surprise, a discovery. If anyone knew who I was or recognized me, they did not say so. Privacy was respected here and politeness was endemic.

There were warm evenings lying on a blanket beneath the stars, making love to Michelle in the garden behind her house. Sometimes Michelle would fall asleep and I'd have to wake her and lead her back to the bedroom. Sometimes in the mornings we'd just sit up in bed and talk.

"What we have for a short while is more than what

some people ever have in a lifetime," she said one morning.

"I know that. But I'm not sure I'll be able to go on after you leave me."

"You will," she said. But I saw the pained look on her face and knew that from then on, I would never speak those words again, no matter what I felt in my heart.

Michelle asked if I would mind if she worked two hours each day with the children—counseling, as she had done before. I told her I was fine with it.

Two weeks later, she told me she wanted me to come to the hospital to meet some of those children.

"I'm not sure I'd be able to do that," I said.

"It's not like you think. Please."

"Okay, I'll come."

There was a little ten-year-old girl and two nine-year-old boys. They seemed perfectly healthy and happy. They seemed normal.

"Susan, Tom, and Gareth," Michelle said. "This is Nigel."

They all smiled. "Wanna play?" Gareth asked.

"Sure."

It had been a long while since I'd been around little kids. I sat down on the floor and Tom poked me in the ribs. "Just wanted to see if you were real," he said.

I poked him back ever so gently. "You real?"

"Uh-huh," he said.

The three of them sat on the floor and I read a really old picture book to them. Michelle left the room as I began. They all laughed at the parts about the skunks.

By the time Michelle returned, they were giggling and telling me their own stories. "Time for a break," she said, which meant it was time for their treatment. A nurse led them out of the room and they each shook my hand and then kissed me on the cheek.

"They seem so healthy. And happy. Do they know?"

"Yes. They know. And I think they understand."

"How can that be?"

"They understand that they have their lives to live each day at a time. They spend time with their parents, they play, they get to know each other and the staff. They have friends and they receive medical care."

"But I don't see any indication of their being in pain."

"In that area, we've made considerable improvements. We can cure more diseases but not all. We extend and improve the quality of life but it has its limitations. In your time, these children would not have made it past three. In our time, children who would have died at birth sometimes live until they are teenagers."

And then she grew silent.

"And you were one of those children?" I asked.

"Yes. I've known for a long time when I was supposed to die. They've stretched the limits for me."

"But you're not in pain? You're like them."

"Remember Jonathan Krieg?"

"Of course."

"He has always been a mystery to just about everyone. If you were writing a book about a utopian future, why was this murderer such an important part of the story?"

"I guess Austin needed difficult challenges, not easy ones. And I wanted to show that all futures were imperfect in some way. And I wanted to show that even a murderer could be someone who had a good heart."

"It was a disturbing aspect of the book. A lot of people are still puzzled by it. But I think that, decades ago, it sparked a controversy and a heightened interest in issues of pain control."

"That was Krieg's expertise."

"Yes. And it prompted people to talk about it much more than before. So several generations were obsessed with eliminating pain—as much as is humanly possible. And like Krieg, some researchers started coming up with hybrid treatments. Combinations of many forms of therapy with fewer and fewer incapacitating drugs. And now we have something in place to allow these kids to live their lives, however short, relatively pain free."

"But you can't cure them?" I asked again.

"Not these ones. And not me."

Chapter Twenty-One

At first I grew to love the world I had moved into. It was not, of course, the future vision I had created in my novel, except for the fact that remarkable young people had a significant number of important jobs. There was no mandatory retirement. Many did serve five or six years at work and then moved on to something else, usually not a form of employment. Others, like Franklin and Mary, continued to "work" at their chosen vocation for years.

Michelle's decline began four months after my arrival. And it was then I began to hate some things about where I was. I hated the fact that everyone, including Franklin and

Mary, *accepted* that Michelle would die. I had already been around for the death of Susan and Tom. Michelle had counseled me on what would happen. The kids themselves had counseled me. "I'm your friend," Tom had said to me the last time I visited him, "so I don't want to do anything to make you sad. So you have to promise me you'll be okay."

I had promised. There was a similar scene with Susan. And I had watched the nurses and doctors treat the children almost as if they were perfectly normal, right up to the time they died. I had watched Michelle deal with it as well. She cared for them and talked openly with them about their death. And when they were gone, she moved on to help the next child.

I had stopped visiting with the children after Susan's death. It was then I became convinced I did not belong in this world.

Mary and Franklin had talked to me about being trained to follow in Michelle's footsteps, to take over her job after she was gone.

But I refused.

Toward the end of the fifth month, Michelle could not work with the children anymore. Franklin and Mary offered to move in with us for the final weeks. But we both said no.

I made the mistake, one day, of opening up the "what if"

conversation with Michelle.

"What if we had never met?"

"Everything would have been different," she said.

"What if you weren't sick?"

"Then we would never have met."

"But what if you didn't have to die?"

Her eyes teared up as she tried to smile. "Then we'd get to live happily ever after."

But I didn't ask any more questions. I was now feeling angry and bitter. I was having a harder and harder time holding onto the joy in the days that were left.

One day, she started to succumb to the pain. She said she wanted to stay with me, that she didn't need to go to the hospital. "I wish I could skip this step," she said.

"What do you mean?"

"There's not anything more that can be done at this point. I could use the heavier drugs. The old ones. And I could drift off. Or I can stay awake and be with you."

"And suffer?"

"Yes."

"Why would you do that?"

"To be with you."

"There's no other way?"

"No."

I'd like to tell you how calm and heroic I was over those next twenty-four hours. I'd like to tell you I did a good job of keeping Michelle's spirits up through the final phase of her illness leading to her death.

But I did not.

She was stronger than me right up to the end. I found myself arguing with her to take the meds—the painkillers. But she said she "understood" about the suffering phase and was prepared for it. It was agreed that I would be the only one there at the end. Michelle had already said her goodbyes to the others.

I lay alongside her as she took her last breath, my arms desperately holding onto the girl I loved, the one I was about to lose.

And then she was gone.

Chapter Twenty-Two

There can be nothing more lonely and sad than to be some-one who has traveled from far, far away to be with someone he loves and then to lose that special someone. When we suffer our losses, we fall back on old, reliable, familiar ways, even if they are poor substitutes. But I had none of that. I was not of this time or this place. And my old familiar things were long, long gone.

I spoke to Franklin about the possibility of my returning to my own time line.

"The Council has decided to put all travel on hold. Everyone agrees that there is so much we don't understand.

Some still debate whether Michelle, Mary, and I should have gone back. The new group in charge thinks there are too many variables. They say that, just because we can do it, it doesn't mean we should. The Council will never agree to let you go back, having seen what you have, having lived among us."

"Then what do I do?"

"Create a life here."

"But I don't think I can do that. I thought I could—or maybe I never really thought about it—but now that she's gone, I'm lost."

"Think beyond the pain. Think of something you would like to do."

I tried to grab onto anything, no matter how trivial. *Something I would like to do.*

"I'd like to die," I said, looking straight at Franklin.

And he did not blink or turn away or say any words to dissuade me.

When you go to the so-called retreat, the first thing they tell you is that you are given permission to die. No one will stop you and you will be assisted with the most painless death possible if you so choose.

But first you must open your mind to other possibilities or, if you refuse, you should work at preparing yourself properly for death. I could have chosen one of the younger retreat counselors to be my guide, as was suggested. But I refused. I asked Franklin to help me. "That may be a mistake," he said, "because I'm also a link to Michelle. And the fact that you can't leave Michelle behind is why you want to die."

"I know," I said. "But I trust you."

He nodded. "Where do we begin?"

"Why do you ask me?"

"Everyone here chooses a path. You have to set the course."

"I would like you to prepare me to die."

"How?"

"Like before. The way you prepared me to be open to new concepts, and then the way Michelle put images in my head that seemed so real. I want you to bring her back to me like that."

"That could be more painful than helpful."

"I don't care," I said.

"Okay."

We were alone in a small geodesic-dome "cabin" in a forest outside the city. I sat quietly and allowed him to guide me through a meditation practice much like before. He was very patient and calm. Nothing much happened the first day or the second. I protested but he said I must be patient.

On the third day, after the moment of the imagined

bright white light shining into my mind, Michelle appeared to me. She looked healthy and beautiful. Her eyes seemed to be looking into my soul. In my mind, I tried to speak but there were no words. I held her image there in my head and ached desperately to touch her physically. And then she moved away. I thought she was leaving but, as she moved away, I saw myself beside her. We were in her garden, the sun out, the flowers blooming. And then she was gone.

After I opened my eyes, I told Franklin what I had seen. "Was this something you put in my head? A kind of project-ed fantasy?"

"I'm not really sure what you experienced. I helped open a pathway, but it is for you to decide if it was real or just a fantasy created by your memory and imagination."

"How can I tell what it is?"

"Does it really matter?" he asked.

Later that day, sitting quietly beneath the trees, I decided it didn't matter. I also saw that if it was me controlling that vision of Michelle, then that was the vision that I would use to guide me to my death.

That evening I asked Franklin about the drugs I could use for the painless death. "Give it more time," he suggested. "Wait for her to return to you several times first."

Out of respect for him, and out of the promise of her returning vision, I agreed. Yet, as Franklin had predicted, the loss seemed sharper now that Michelle had appeared to me. I felt calmer, however, and prepared myself to continue the meditative training like this for many more days.

Each day, Franklin coached me into ever deeper states of meditation. Each time, Michelle would eventually appear to me in a familiar setting—the garden, her kitchen, her bedroom. Each time it would seem more real. We would talk. I would hold her. I would awake afterwards and Franklin would sometimes be gone and it would be night.

Then one morning, Franklin explained about the various methods approved by the retreat for self-administered death. The simplest was a pill. One swallow with a glass of water. Not much to it. I asked for this to be delivered the following day.

And my wish was granted without protest. A small white dish with a grey pill and a glass of water was delivered. "Would you like me to stay?" Franklin asked.

"No," I said. "I'll meditate for a while ... and then go from there."

He bowed slightly and then left the room.

He left me alone and I settled into a seated meditative position. The darkness and then the light, the feeling of being outside of my body—this time even looking down at myself meditating, from above, as if I were hovering. And then waiting for Michelle to appear.

I saw her walking towards me down a brightly lit hallway that I did not recognize at first. She was smiling, happy to see me. Again, she looked healthy and so alive. When she took my hand, I understood where we were. We were in the hospital.

It was such a warm and cheerful place that I didn't mind being there. She led me into a room and we both sat down on the floor. I kissed her lightly on the lips and then a door opened. Susan, Tom, and Gareth ran into the room towards us. They hugged Michelle and then threw their arms around me. I felt their joy and their playful spirit. And then the door opened again and more children poured into the room. As each one entered, I sensed the room getting brighter and warmer. I sensed the life energy of each new child who entered, until the room was filled with many children. Michelle and I were sitting in the center.

And then the room went quiet. Michelle stood up and took my hand to stand with her as well. She looked deep into my eyes and I felt her warmth within me now.

As she walked out of the room, I began to understand. She was leaving, but within my heart, I felt she was still there. The children were silent and smiling.

And then I opened my eyes.

Once again I was alone in my dark room. But I was standing up. At first I felt terrifyingly alone. I did not understand why that had happened and why everything had dropped away so quickly. I cried out. A sound. A lonely, plaintive wail. But if anyone heard, no one came to me. I was still alone.

I turned on a small lamp that I found by groping along the table, and then I saw the drug and the glass of water. I let out another sound, a sigh this time, an exhalation coming from so deep within that when I sucked in my next breath, it was as if I were breathing in a massive flood of oxygen.

And then I left the cabin and walked out into the night. When I looked up, I discovered the dark night sky was filled with hundreds of bright stars, each one of them reminding me of a child I had just seen in my vision. And I heard the voice of Michelle speaking to me, telling me that this was the world where I now belonged, where she had prepared me to continue with the work that was yet to be done.

Interview with Lesley Choyce

What prompted you to write this book?

Sometimes I get the feeling that we are wasting valuable talent—young people with extraordinary skills and abilities that have not been given the opportunity to use them. So I posed this big "what if?" question to myself. The story flowed from there. Adults have not been that good at solving some of the world's greatest problems—war, poverty, prejudice etc. Why not let young people with possibly some radical new improved ideas take over?

In your story, Gary says: "So-called laws created to protect kids have instead imprisoned them." You suggest that teenagers are, in a sense, prevented from contributing to society in a significant way. Tell me about that.

When I was a teenager, I think I was operating at about twenty percent of my ability. And I was not alone. As adults, we want to protect our kids but fail most of the time to allow them to live up to their abilities as a result. They need to take risks and often take the wrong risks. We need to present them with real opportunities to live up to their potential.

Do you think that really bright kids are discriminated against in the school system now? Why does that happen?

Really smart kids are bored to death by most schooling. They should be offered a wide range of opportunities to explore what they want to explore, not just what's in the curriculum. They need to be encouraged to do this and rewarded accordingly. When it comes to environmental issues for instance, they often profess radical changes and we should maybe listen.

Most adults are afraid of new ideas and big changes and the thought of kids with smarts gaining power scares adults. So we hold kids back. Some of them survive, some go crazy, some look for trouble. In a way, they should be put to work at something they love and be productive.

Why do you think some people in the story are angry at the suggestions made in Nigel's novel?

Fear of change. They cling to old beliefs even if those old beliefs are no longer fair or functional.

How do you think it is that the world Nigel envisions in his novel could occur?

It is not likely to occur as set out in the book. But we will move in that direction if we are smart. Give young people more voice, more political power, more opportunity to really move us into the future in a smart way.

Is this the first time you have written a novel which is partly based in fantasy? What drew you to this genre in this case?

I started out writing science fiction as a teenager. I've published two science fiction/fantasy novels for adults and one (*Deconstructing Dylan*) set in the future. I've just finished editing a book called *Nova Scotia: Visions of the Future* that includes forty writers describing their visions for this province. I'm concerned about how lazy *we* are when *we* contemplate the future. We need to make some really big moves to redistribute the wealth, the power, the knowledge and stop wasting money on waging war and rewarding greed.

What advice would you give young writers?

Make the leap. Write what needs to be written. Speak brave new words and new ideas. Write from the heart and avoid trying to fit into a current trend or fad. The world needs gutsy realistic fiction that faces up to the reality of the world we live in and the one we will be living in. Writing should also be an adventure of the heart and mind for the person creating it. If what you are writing makes you sweat that is a good sign. If it makes you ache, that is good too. You'll need to laugh out loud at some of what you write and you'll need to scare yourself by being so daring and true.

You're an adult: a father, an author and publisher—and you've had many adventures. Would it be true to say that, despite this, there's still a sixteen-year-old deep inside trying to figure out what to do with your life, how to deal with the world? Is that what makes you so interested in writing books for teenagers?

I still wake up every morning asking myself the same damn question: "Who am I now?" I have some kind of fix on who I was yesterday or ten years ago or when I was young but now remains a mystery. In that regard, I'm still mid teen. I work my hunches and pretend I know what I'm doing but, like a sixteen-year-old, I'm still trying to figure things out and determine where I fit in—or, more often than not, discovering I don't really fit in. I keep thinking that I will one day conform to the world but mostly have given up on that, so my alternate plan is for the world to conform to me. Don't know if this will happen, though.

I just know that I need all those adventures with more to come and many of them to take place as I write my next book.

Thank you, Lesley.

Lesley Choyce once said that a voice in his head told him:
"Write about what makes you feel the most uncomfortable."
Lesley is an award-winning author of 65 books for children,
teens and adults. He's also a musician, publisher, and broadcaster
who surfs year-round in the North Atlantic and
teaches at Dalhousie University.
Lesley lives in Halifax.